Praise for...

"...a ....
that had me sitting on the edge of my seat and eagerly awaiting the next installment." - *Refracted Light Young Adult Book Reviews*

"Do not make any plans on the day you begin, as once you start, you will not be able to put it down." - *L.M. Stull, Author*

"Forbidden Mind is beautifully written and worth your reading time." - *BookWormSans*

Incredible Raves for *Forbidden Fire* (Forbidden #2)

"Forbidden Fire is explosive! It's action-packed, riveting and so full of surprises you never would have seen coming! Get ready to be on Fire because this is one book that you will never ever forget!!!" - *Amy Conley*

"Kimberly's amazing writing brought my desire to read back to life. The twists and turns will keep you guessing and at the edge of your seat wanting more. It is now one of my most favorite books." - *Jessica Marr*

"Action, action, and more action. That's what this second book in the series is all about! This story is full of action on every page. And the ending - Wow! I loved the ending of this book! Talk about ending with a bang and lots of twists." -*Wall-to-Wall Books*

Other Books by Kimberly Kinrade

The Forbidden Trilogy
Forbidden Mind
Forbidden Fire
Forbidden Life *

The Three Lost Kids
Lexie World
Bella World
Maddie World*
The Death of the Sugar Fairy*
The Christmas Curse*
Cupid's Capture*

The Reluctant Familiar
The Reluctant Familiar*
The Egyptian Queen (a prequel)*

The Chronicles of Corinne
Death by Destiny*
Myths of Magic*
Paths to Power*

The Fallen Trilogy
Blood of the Fallen (with Dmytry Karpov)*
Sunrise & Nightfall (with Dmytry Karpov)*

Bits of You & Pieces of Me

*Coming Soon from Evolved Publishing

FORBIDDEN MIND

KIMBERLY KINRADE

12.7.12

*To Ethen

Merry Christmas

♡ Kimberly
Kinrade*

P.S. Read this one first!

FORBIDDEN MIND
Copyright © 2012 by Kimberly Kinrade
Cover Art Copyright © 2012 by Sarah E. Melville

All rights reserved. Printed in the United States of America. No part of this book may be used or reproduced in any manner whatsoever, without written permission, except in the case of brief quotations embedded in articles and reviews. For information, contact Evolved Publishing via e-mail at Publisher@EvolvedPub.com.

SECOND EDITION
ISBN: 1622530004
ISBN-13: 978-1-62253-000-7
ASIN: B005LSDIYG

Edited by Lane Diamond and John Allen

Printed in the U.S.A.

www.evolvedpub.com
Evolved Publishing LLC
Rome, Georgia

Forbidden Mind is a work of fiction. All names, characters, places, and incidents are the product of the author's imagination, or are used fictitiously. Any resemblance to actual events or persons, living or dead, is entirely coincidental.

Printed in Book Antiqua font.

*For Dmytry Karpov,
who gave me the inspiration
to write fiction again and who helps me brainstorm,
edit and format every book I write.
I love you.*

Table of Contents

CHAPTER 1 – SAM
One more stroke of red and… 1
CHAPTER 2 – SAM
The Hub occupied prime real estate… 10
CHAPTER 3 – DRAKE
Warm rays of sun beat down… 17
CHAPTER 4 – SAM
Music blared from Luke and Lucy's suite… ..30
CHAPTER 5 – DRAKE
At four in the morning… 38
CHAPTER 6 – SAM
The next morning… 45
CHAPTER 7 – SAM
For a man who'd hardly been home… 52
CHAPTER 8 – DRAKE
When Drake regained some semblance… 63
CHAPTER 9 – SAM
No matter how many times I'd… 65
CHAPTER 10 – SAM
Luke walked through my door… 75
CHAPTER 11 – DRAKE
Awareness flickered in and out… 84
CHAPTER 12 – SAM
Sleep came slowly that night… 89
CHAPTER 13 – SAM
"Luke, Lucy, open up!" 105
CHAPTER 14 – SAM
Two days of forced bed rest… 113
CHAPTER 15 – SAM
Over the next few weeks, dizziness… 123
CHAPTER 16 – SAM
Dr. Sato didn't release me from the Clinic ...129
CHAPTER 17 – SAM
The car slowed to a stop… 144

CHAPTER 18 – SAM
I fought against the consciousness… 158
CHAPTER 19 – SAM
I tried to infuse my mental voice… 166
CHAPTER 20 – SAM
Our plan should have been simple 177
CHAPTER 21 – SAM
I'd never expected to play hero… 183
Chapter 22 – SAM
We had little time left 191
CHAPTER 23 – SAM
Drake and I linked and commanded… 200
CHAPTER 24 – DRAKE
Drake cradled Ana's head… 204
CHAPTER 25 – SAM
I heard the gun explode in slow motion 208

ACKNOWLEDGEMENTS 219
ABOUT THE AUTHOR 222
WHAT'S NEXT 224
Other Novels From Evolved Publishing 236

This Page Intentionally Left Blank

CHAPTER 1 – SAM

One more stroke of red... and done! My cramped fingers reluctantly released the paintbrush. After six hours of non-stop painting, no part of my body wanted to move, but all of it needed to. When in the zone, I never felt the strain of time—only *after* the project did it catch up to me, the aching muscles and burning pain in my hand, the serious need to pee.

I darted for the bathroom attached to the art studio, but nearly tripped over my still-asleep legs when they failed to move as instructed. With a groan and a very full bladder, I lumbered in and relieved myself, then returned to my easel and stretched all of my angry muscles.

A deep voice startled me out of my back stretch. "Wow, Sam, this has got to be your best work yet." Mr. Krevner, Mr. K for short, stood in a shadowed corner of the studio and stared at my painting.

I'd never seen him so enraptured by any of my work. I'd never seen him speechless before, either, and that stroked my artistic ego as nothing else could. The 16x24 canvas oil painting that had stolen my social life for the past two months radiated an aliveness and color that I'd never been able to capture before.

My art professor came forward, walking as though in a church and speaking in a hushed voice. "Where did you get the inspiration for this? The layers of texture and use of tone are extraordinary, and the juxtaposition of fluid brush strokes and harsh, jagged lines creates a dynamic movement to the piece, a conflict that has been missing in your other work. Extraordinary. What are you calling it?"

The hitch in my voice betrayed my nerves. "The Color of Thought. It represents how I 'see' the world, with the thoughts of everyone swirling around me, and the conflict I feel at having so many minds invade my own. I went with a more abstract style to capture the frenetic energy of my experiences. I know my work is usually more realistic, but...."

Nothing in my art had ever been so personal. Maybe great art had to be ripped from a person's soul, before it could evoke emotion in others.

"Do you think it's good enough for the International Art Contest?" I dipped into his thoughts, but he spoke exactly what was on his mind.

His long fingers intertwined, and his thin, penciled-in eyebrows shot up and down in excitement. "Good enough? It's better than that. It's incredible! In two weeks, you'll be the winner of one of the most prestigious art contests in the world. It'll make your career and get you into Sarah Lawrence."

I covered my painting with a piece of canvas, careful not to touch the wet paint, scrubbed my hands and brushes in the sink, and grabbed my book bag. "I haven't even gotten accepted yet."

He walked me to the door. "You will. Don't worry about it. Your future is assured."

I adjusted my backpack onto my shoulders. "I'm going to get something to eat. I'll come back later to talk about the contest details with you."

When Mr. K smiled, his hawk nose and skeletal facial features transformed into something less reminiscent of Jack Skellington from *The Nightmare Before Christmas*—his usual look. He was almost, for just a moment, handsome—though not my type at all. Way too old.

"Enjoy your dinner, Sam." He walked back into the studio, his long scarecrow body swimming in his khakis and Grateful Dead t-shirt.

The great clock above the Headmaster's building chimed four times. Where would Lucy and Luke be this fine Saturday? I cocked my head and listened for their mental signatures, but a blast of unwelcome thoughts barraged me.

'Can't believe I have to study today.... Where is my sock...? Really need to get this fire under control.... Wish the weekend would last longer....'

Our secret school for kids with para-powers only had about 500 students, grades seven to twelve, but that's still a lot of minds to wade through. Finally, Lucy's distinctive mental voice pierced through the rest.

I stood on the southeast end of campus, where a cluster of classrooms made up the fine arts department. Each building on our campus looked like a small mansion that had transported itself from the Tudor period in England. The meticulous landscaping, complete with bushes trimmed into animal shapes, reinforced the illusion of a proper English estate. Only the high voltage fences surrounding the perimeter spoiled the effect.

The winding cobblestone path led me west from the studio toward the phys ed building and training courtyard. Spring hadn't yet given way to summer, but today felt like a small victory over a long winter. I basked in the warmth of the sun as I looked for my best friends.

I knew what I'd see upon arriving, and wasn't disappointed.

A small crowd had formed around the outdoor training court, where layers of mats lay on the ground and my two favorite people stood center stage. Lucy had her much bigger and taller twin brother, Luke, in a chokehold, from which he struggled to remove himself. Students passed small wads of cash back and forth, clearly betting on the winner. When Luke flipped Lucy on her back and pinned her petite frame to the mat, those who had bet on Luke started cheering.

They didn't know Lucy.

And I wished I'd brought some cash.

She scissored her legs around her brother's neck and flipped herself up so that she straddled his throat. Incredible! With another hip move, she knocked him down and pinned him for the count.

Students cheered and exchanged money as she stood and offered her hand to him. He grudgingly accepted, and they pushed through the crowds, finally spotting me.

Luke draped his long arm over my shoulder. His blue eyes twinkled even as he moaned and groaned in mock abuse. "Did you see what this pint-sized maniac did to me? Appalling."

I laughed and tugged at Lucy's dark ponytail. "You sure showed him. Of course, you've been showing him up since kindergarten."

Luke stuck his tongue at me and Lucy flashed her 100-watt smile. "Did you finish? Do I finally get to see this super-secret painting that has kept you in hermit mode for months?"

My grin spread into a full-on face-cramping smile. "It's done! And it's... I can't even explain. It's the best thing I've ever painted!"

They both grabbed my arms and pulled me back to the studio. "We want to see it now!" they said in unison.

"But I'm so hungry. I haven't eaten all day." They ignored my pleas as we retraced my steps.

As much as my rumbling stomach needed food, I was way more excited to share my work with my friends. I hadn't shown it to anyone while I worked, and being out of the loop never sat well with my feisty friends. Plus, they deserved to be a part of this after encouraging me for years to pursue my art more seriously. Lucy had actually used her very first bonus from an assignment to commission a portrait from me. How could I deny my first paying customer—especially since most of the students at the school now had my art hanging in their rooms, and I had a nice stash of cash in mine, thanks to her and Luke?

***

The door to the studio hung open just a crack, and angry screams assaulted us as we approached. Luke and Lucy looked to me as if I knew what was going on.

I shrugged my shoulders in the universal I've-got-no-freaking-idea way and crept to the door. I could have just slipped into their minds, but listening to people talk both out load and mentally was hard to track and gave me a pretty big headache. At that moment, what they were saying, or rather screaming, to each other was more interesting.

We didn't want to budge the door and draw attention to ourselves, so Luke pushed his head through. He bobbed in and out so quickly I almost missed it. Being able to walk through anything was mighty handy at times.

I nudged him. "Well?"

"Higgins and Mr. K. They both look pretty pissed."

They sounded it too. I'd never heard Headmaster Higgins yell at any of the teachers, or students for that matter. He wasn't a pushover by any stretch, but he'd always been levelheaded—until today.

Higgins shouted at Mr. K. "How could you enter her without permission from me? Do you realize what you've done? This could ruin the school and everything we're doing here."

Was Higgins talking about me?

Mr. K replied with the same volume and anger. I could imagine the vein over his left eye bulging. "You have no idea how talented that girl is! She should be at the best art school in the world, not hidden here like a freak of nature. It's my job to make sure she has a future when she leaves this god-awful place, and I'm not letting you, or the people you work for, stand in my way. Or hers."

They must have been talking about me, but it made no sense. Why didn't Higgins want me entering the contest, and why did Mr. K hate this place so much?

"Don't you mean, the people *we* work for? They employ us both, and you'd do well to remember that, Mr. Krevner. Their reach extends beyond the gates of this school."

I couldn't believe it. Was the headmaster actually threatening my art teacher? What was going on?

"You will pull her from that competition and clean up the mess you've made, or your days here are numbered. Am I making myself clear?"

Something crashed into a wall, and my friends and I jumped back in surprise.

"Everything is very clear. You use her and her gifts, rent her and all these kids out to the highest bidder as spies. You make billions on these Rent-A-Kids, as they call themselves. And now you want to snuff her chance to shine doing what she truly loves? No. If you want to destroy her dreams, you can do it yourself. I'll have no part in it."

Footsteps approached the door. I tripped back, grabbed Luke and Lucy, and the three of us ducked around the corner of the building. I peeked out just as Mr. K stormed from the studio, his face bright red and contorted in anger. Not his best look.

Headmaster Higgins followed him out moments later. He adjusted his navy blue suit and plastered a calm mask over his face. His midnight black skin did not reveal his recent spike in blood pressure the same way that Mr. K's pasty complexion had, but the tight way he held his shoulders and the fists he made of his hands spoke to his anger.

Tears stung my eyes, and I swiped at them with the back of a hand still stained with splashes of paint. If they pulled me from the contest, hundreds of hours of hard work would be wasted, and my future would get flushed down the toilet. That couldn't happen!

When both men were gone, the three of us snuck into the studio and closed the door behind us. My enthusiasm had drained out of me like dirty bathtub water. I sniffled and wiped my traitorous eyes again.

Lucy put her arm around me. "Cheer up, Chica. We'll figure this out, I promise. They can't keep you from this, not after all the hard work you've done. And you'll be leaving for New York soon. Luke and I will join you there, and we'll make all of our dreams come true, just watch!"

I tried to smile, for her sake, but the smile didn't reach my eyes.

Luke rubbed my head as if I were his pet dog. "Where's this painting I've been hearing so little about?"

I swatted his hand and couldn't suppress a small, but genuine, smile. Luke could always cheer me: funny, gorgeous, and so much like a brother it sucked.

"Over here." The canvas draped over my painting appeared undisturbed. A sigh of relief escaped me. At least nothing had happened to it. "Close your eyes."

They both groaned but did as told.

Fear and nervousness buzzed through me as I pulled the canvas off. What if they hated it? What if everyone hated it and my dreams of being a real artist died before they could even be born? My lungs clenched with stale breath and I exhaled before I got too dizzy. "Okay, you can look."

They stood there, jaws dropped, stunned into silence. They either hated it or totally loved it.

"Um, is this a bad or good silence?"

Lucy pulled her mouth closed and swallowed before she spoke. "O.M.G. Sam, this is the most incredible, unbelievable thing I've ever seen in my life. You painted this?"

"You like it?"

Her mental voice slammed into me. *'Would I lie to you? It's amazing!'*

Relief flooded me even as I laughed at her joke. I could read minds, sure, but she was the human lie detector. No one dared lie to her.

Luke hugged me and whispered into my ear, "I'm so proud of you, Sam. This is truly epic!"

We stood there staring for several minutes. This painting represented so much about me, my life, my future... everything. I hated to leave it even for a minute, but my stomach protested its neglect with a loud rumble.

Luke grabbed my hand. "Come on, let's feed you. My treat."

With the buzz of success filling me, and Luke's hand in mine, I entertained a what-if. What if I could get past the whole brother thing with Luke? I took in his tall, well-defined frame, his dark hair and bright blue eyes. Gorgeous inside and out, but... nothing. No spark at all. Such a pity. Of all the guys at school, he was the only one I could even imagine being with, but I couldn't force the chemistry and neither could he.

We walked to dinner hand in hand, and I consoled myself with the fact that I had the best friends a girl could want. Not a bad consolation prize after all, and worth a hundred boyfriends.

CHAPTER 2 – SAM

The Hub occupied prime real estate in the middle of campus and offered the only thing that passed for excitement at our school. On such a beautiful day, every shop and cafe was open for business. The Hub was our little town, the only place we had to buy clothes, food, knickknacks and whatever else we needed. If a store didn't have what we wanted, they'd order it.

We walked down the tree-lined sidewalks and looked for a restaurant that had space for us. Three girls from my math class were just getting up to leave as we approached The Bistro, a fun deli that served the best meatball subs. We snagged the table and settled in for a much needed meal.

The waitress took our order promptly, probably trying to get people in and out as quickly as possible for more tips. Luke sipped his soda with over-the-top slurping noises.

"Honestly, you are such a pig, Luke."

He threw his wadded-up straw paper at me. "Whatcha gonna do about it, pip squeak?"

I stuck my tongue at him, then settled into a sulk, arms crossed over my chest. "What am I going to do if Higgins pulls me from the contest?"

Lucy's brown eyes blazed with fire. "He wouldn't dare! You've worked too hard for that. And Mr. K won't let him pull you. I think he'd crawl across sharp glass all the way to New York with your painting strapped to his back if he had to, just to make sure you were entered. Honestly, I think the only reason he still teaches here is because of you."

"He does seem really unhappy. Why do you think he hates it here so much?" I looked around at the palatial grounds and happy students strolling the streets. We had everything we could ever need. Sure, it got boring and lonely sometimes, but the occasional assignment to places all over the world kept things interesting and made coming home a nice change of pace. Why would he want to leave?

Our meals arrived, and talking ceased as we all took big bites of our sandwiches.

The warm meatballs and toasted honey and oat bread had never tasted better, and filling my stomach helped settle the shaky energy of too much caffeine the last two days.

Lucy talked through a mouth full of roasted turkey breast. "Who knows, but it's not so crazy, is it? I mean how badly do *we* want to leave?"

"That's different. We all have para-powers that make us vulnerable in the real world, and make some of us dangerous. We're here to learn to control our powers and to protect us from those who might exploit us. We have no choice, at least until we turn eighteen and are finally free."

Lucy rolled her eyes. "We all know the company line, Sam."

The waitress came and refilled our drinks, and I used the interruption to organize my thoughts and take another bite of my sandwich.

Out of habit, I peeked into the waitress's mind and smirked. *'So sexy... wish I could get him to notice me... wish we were allowed to date the students....'*

When she left I kicked Luke under the table. "You're charming the ladies and don't even know it." I nodded toward the waitress.

He puffed up his chest and raised a "how you doin'" eyebrow. "Girls just can't help but appreciate all that I have to offer. And who can blame them, really?"

"Yes, such a ladies' man. Anyways, I know it's not easy for our teachers. It's just... as far as schools go, they've got it pretty good. I mean, we've all had to go to other schools while on assignment, and they suck compared to this. The teachers are miserable, underpaid and overworked, and there are too many students per classroom. Here he gets state-of-the-art equipment, any kind of supplies he wants, and an incredible studio. Why leave?"

Luke paused from inhaling his bacon burger long enough to respond. "True. Some of those schools are scary. Don't know how anyone learns anything. But who knows? Maybe he just doesn't like how secluded we are or that he has to keep secrets about where he works and what he does. I doubt any teacher here has much of a life off campus, ya know?"

I finished my last bite of sandwich and wiped the extra marinara sauce off my lips with a napkin. "I'm going to go talk to Higgins. I can't lose this chance."

Lucy picked a stray piece of turkey from her plate and plopped it into her mouth. "Do you want us to come? Moral support? Back up? Whatever."

"Nah, you two need showers after all your sparring. I'll be okay. When I'm done I'll find you in your suite."

Luke left money for our dinner and the tip, and they walked back to the dorms while I headed to Higgins's office. Normally he took the weekends off, but I had a suspicion he'd be there today. The main offices took up the northwest corner of campus, shaped like a square, and surrounded by an electrified fence and a brick wall with tall trees cloaking the outside.

We'd gone off school grounds on field trips for survival training, and while I didn't know what state we were in—or even what country—I did know that we were surrounded by woods. Lots of woods. My guess? Our locale felt distinctly North American, though I couldn't pinpoint exactly why. The weather made me think Pacific Northwest, or Midwest, with the seasonal changes and landscape.

I walked past the gate that served as the only entrance or exit on campus and waved at the guard, Old Charlie, a staple at Rent-A-Kid who always treated us well. He smiled and waved back. He looked harmless, but he'd done some demonstrations for us in martial arts. Even Luke and Lucy, who put my sad excuse for combat skills to shame, bowed to his ninja ways. It had always made me feel safe, knowing Old Charlie was standing guard, protecting us from anyone who might discover our secret location and cause us harm.

The shadows of twilight cloaked the offices, and none of the lights inside appeared to be on. I turned the knob, relieved to find it unlocked, and let myself in.

Higgins's voice carried from his office—no responses, so he must have been on the phone.

I opened my mind and pressed into his thoughts.

'Damage control... Must contain this situation before it gets to the top... Damn Krevner, should never have hired him... Always has been a renegade... What to tell Sam?'

When he hung up, I knocked on his door.

"Who is it?"

"It's Sam. Can I talk to you?"

'Crap! Not ready to deal with her.' "Can this wait?"

"Um, not really. Can I come in?"

'Damn Krevner.' "Sure, come on in."

Higgins's office, normally so meticulous, from the always clean and empty trashcan to the perfectly placed pens and pencils, was surprisingly messy. Crumpled papers covered his desk, his suit jacket slouched in a pile on the floor like a deflated man, and his tie hung down his chest at an odd angle, as if he'd been pulling at it. He ran his hands through his greying hair, and I could see his toned muscles flex under his shirt. For someone in his fifties, he was pretty cut.

"Sam, I'm actually glad you came. I have an assignment for you."

This was unexpected. "Headmaster Higgins, I really can't go on assignment right now. I have the art contest to prep for, an interview with Sarah Lawrence coming up, and homework. I'm swamped."

'What do I do about this damn art contest? How do I get out of this?'

"You know I can read your mind, right? I also overheard you and Mr. K screaming at each other. Actually, I'm surprised the whole school didn't hear. You can't pull me from the contest. I have to be in it! I've worked so hard on this painting, and if I win, Sarah Lawrence is guaranteed. So is my career."

He nervously shuffled his hands back and forth, then put them on his lap when he saw me looking. "I'm sorry, Sam, but it's too much exposure for the school. We have to keep a low profile to keep you all safe. How do we explain who you are or where you're from if you win?"

Tightness formed in my chest. "You create believable false identities for us every time we leave this campus. Why can't you use my new identity, the one I'll be using at Sarah Lawrence? I'm assuming their admissions department has some fake history for me there, right? So I become *her*, whoever she is, and I take on that role like any other assignment. It doesn't seem like it would be that hard."

"I'll give it some thought and see what we can do, okay? But only if you agree to take this assignment. It just came in. It's an important client and it has your name, and para-power, written all over it."

He scooted a file across the desk and I flipped through it while he gave me a verbal briefing. "Henry Dollinger needs dirt on his business partner, Ronald Beaumont, so he can force a buy-out and take control of the company. He knows Beaumont is hiding something, but can't figure out what."

"You want me to crack open his mind and dig out his secrets."

Higgins's chair squeaked as he sat back. "Yes. You leave on Tuesday. We're putting together your identity now."

"What? My interview with Sarah Lawrence is on Friday. I'll never have enough time to get there, do this job and get back."

"It shouldn't take you that long to get what you need. And while you're gone, I'll do everything I can to keep you in the art contest. Deal?"

I'd never turned down an assignment before, and I was within my rights to do so now, but the potential consequences scared me. At the very least, I'd lose all chance of being in the contest.

Even as my head nodded yes, my gut screamed no. Everything about this felt off.

"Oh, and I'll be sending a guard with you."

"Why?" I scratched at the hidden tracking device in my upper arm. "You always know where I am. It's not like I can get lost or kidnapped."

"It's not that. Another organization has formed, a group bent on destroying anyone with para-powers. They've killed several teens and children in random attacks. I just want to make sure you're safe."

My heart skipped a beat. I knew that kids with para-powers were at risk without Rent-A-Kid, but not that someone was aggressively attacking, and killing, them. Still, a guard?

"How will I explain it?"

"It's part of your cover. You're the daughter of Dollinger's college roommate. Your father is powerful and has enemies, and your life has been threatened. You're staying with Dollinger, under guard, while your family deals with the threats."

I nodded. "Makes sense. Okay, I'll go on Tuesday, but I need to be back by Thursday. It's important."

"We'll be ready to retrieve you when you complete the mission. Now, if there's nothing else...."

I knew a dismissal when I heard one.

While leaving the office, I slipped back into his mind, but he blocked me by silently reciting Shakespeare sonnets over and over.

What was Higgins afraid of thinking? What did he not want me to know?

My gut tightened.

CHAPTER 3 – DRAKE

Warm rays of sun beat down on Drake's back as he leaned over his board. He waited — one breath, then another, inhaling and exhaling to the pulse of the ocean, each swell matching the beat of his heart. All thought, all anger, and all distraction fled in the tranquility of the Pacific, the only place that could bring him peace. He found his God here, his religion. Not even Father Patrick's pews could compete.

The wave approached, and Drake, one with it, stood on his board and sliced through the tide. He balanced on the edge of the world, no longer affected by the push and pull of the needy masses. Sprays of saltwater splashed his face — a baptism for a man who belonged nowhere.

A tingle of dread broke through his zone. It started in his spine and worked its way up his back. He felt sinister eyes on him.

Drake never used his powers while surfing; he didn't need to. But now, he broke his own rule and snaked his mind over the water and to the beach, seeking the person who didn't belong. Nothing felt out of the ordinary, but the break in concentration stole the joy from his meditation.

Anger boiled in his blood, unwilling to be cooled by the water. He turned his board toward the sand and rode back to shore, scanning as he did for anyone paying too much attention to him.

Kylie the Beach Bunny scampered up to him and threw her slender arms around his neck as he shrugged out of his wetsuit. "You looked so hot out there, Drakey. Did you come back for some fun in the sun?" Her lips sought his, but he pulled away.

"Not now, Kylie. I have to get going. Did you see anyone around the beach watching me, or anyone who looked suspicious?"

Her painted, puckered lips turned down in confusion. "No, why? Let's go get a drink and maybe go back to my place if you're done here. I can take your mind off whatever is worrying you. Did you get my text messages and voicemails? I even came by your place but you weren't home. I've missed you." She ran a finger down his wet chest, tracing a drop of water to his navel.

He pulled her hand away. "I said, not now." He added just a bit of compulsion to his voice, using his mind to nudge hers. A vacant expression crossed through her blue eyes then disappeared. He hadn't really controlled her mind; he'd just given it extra encouragement so he could get rid of her without a scene.

Another trickle of foreboding crawled over his shoulders. Goose bumps formed on his arms and he shivered despite the heat.

Kylie frowned, but said nothing else as she walked away, her long, tanned and very exposed body attracting the admiring glances of every man on the beach.

Drake didn't care.

Another, more powerful pricking alerted him to danger. He whipped his head around in time to see a figure in black slip into a car parked in the lot, and drive away.

***

Before anyone else could stop him, Drake grabbed his towel and board and walked the few blocks through the streets of Venice Beach back to his apartment.

His best friend Brad was still asleep, probably up late again—writing, trying to become a famous journalist, but getting stuck with Crime Watch and Feature Obits.

Drake showered, dressed and started a breakfast of bacon and eggs.

Percolating coffee and the smell of frying food finally convinced Brad to join the land of the living. "Dude, you get up way too freaking early."

"You sleep in way too freaking late. On this, we will just have to agree to disagree. Eat some bacon." Drake pushed a plateful of food in front of Brad.

"Thanks, man. How were the waves this morning? You ready for the West Coast Championships?" Brad shoveled breakfast into his mouth.

Drake considered how much he should reveal about his unnerving morning. "I think I'm being watched."

This put a halt to the eating. "Oh, man, I told you this was a bad idea. You need to keep a low profile, dude. Stick to teaching surfing lessons to wannabes, but don't enter an international surfing competition with major media coverage. What if someone finds you?"

The small two-bedroom apartment they shared felt even smaller. Drake fought the urge to escape back into his ocean, but even that holy place had been violated.

He put his dishes in the sink and paced the living room, staring at the stains in the brown carpet. Their bachelor pad wouldn't impress many women, but it kept Drake close to the beach and Brad close to the newspaper he worked for. A happy compromise.

"This is important to me, you know that. I can't spend my life as a beach bum teaching surfing. I want so much more than that. I could get sponsors and surf for a living."

He sighed and sank into the living room chair. A pile of bills taunted him from the coffee table. He shuffled through them, then held them up as evidence. "Phone bills, rent, power, car insurance... by the time I finish paying these every month, I have nothing left. I can't live like this, man."

Brad frowned. "I know what it's like. I'm in the same boat. You'll find a way."

Drake slammed his fist into the table. "No, you're not. You're in a boat going somewhere. You have dreams, ambition, and a way of making it happen. You have family who give a crap about you. What do I have? A shady past, a string of foster parents who only wanted me for the money, and one skill that I can actually use in public. I'm in a sinking boat. I have to find a way to make my life matter. Don't you get that?"

His fist throbbed for a moment, but then his body healed even that, leaving him numb once again.

Brad had been with him through a lot, but he'd never understand where Drake had come from and what he needed. Not totally.

"Drake, you're right. I can't ever know what it's been like for you, but I do know you have to stay low on the radar if you don't want people digging into your past, into what happened when you were young. There are bad people out there who would just love to capture someone with your powers. I don't want to find your name on my next Crime Watch list."

"No one held me responsible for what happened. No one could know. Besides, am I supposed to stay in the shadows on the off chance someone connects my surfing to a sealed file from fourteen years ago?"

Brad washed both of their dishes and spread out on their beige couch, his long limbs draping over the edge. "Maybe you're right. I don't know, dude. I guess it's possible it was just a fluke, that it was just a sponsor checking you out."

"Maybe." But probably not. The presence Drake had felt didn't strike him as friendly or curious. Someone was after him, but who? And why? Could someone have found out about his powers?

He grabbed his keys from the hook hanging by the front door. "I'm going to talk to Father Patrick. Maybe he has some ideas about all this. Plus, I promised Mrs. Maypol I'd help her move some of the garden statues around."

Brad got up and pulled his laptop from the computer bag he kept by the couch. "Be careful, man. And tell Father Patrick I said hi."

Drake closed the door behind him and left Brad to his writing.

***

St. Michael's Catholic Church in Venice had become a second home to Drake, ever since his fifth foster family had taken him there once for an Easter sermon. The stained glass windows and colorful gardens guarded by Angels had stirred a longing in him—not like the ocean, which even at ten years old had stolen his heart—with its own power.

The real draw, however, turned out to be the old priest, Father Patrick.

Drake parked on Naples, and walked around the corner toward the large carved oak door, which had never been locked for as long as Drake could remember.

A young Mexican woman pushed a cart full of fresh tamales down Coeur D'Alene Avenue and, on impulse, Drake stopped her and bought three: one for himself, and one each for Father Patrick and Mrs. Maypol. He smiled at the thought of them enjoying an unexpected treat.

The girl, thinking he'd meant his smile for her, smiled back and lowered her eyes. "Gracias."

"De nada y gracias." He took a bite of the first tamale. "Muy bueno."

Her smile brightened, and she honked the bike horn on her cart and walked on.

Drake ate his tamale in a few large bites, happy that he'd brightened her day a bit too, and walked into the church with the other two tamales palmed in his hand.

He expected to see Father Patrick shuffle down the aisle to greet him, but the old man was nowhere to be seen. A feeling of serenity settled on Drake as he breathed in the stillness of the room. The sea had a constant pulsing energy that soothed, but here the quiet and calm had its own effect on his racing mind.

He made the sign of the cross and kneeled out of habit. While not religious, it didn't hurt to honor the ways of his friend while in his church.

The stained glass windows depicting biblical scenes shone down on him rays of rainbow light. He imagined the halo effect that anyone looking at him just then would see—not that he'd ever be mistaken for someone holy. Still, he liked to imagine his soul could be redeemed, someday, by someone who saw in him what Father Patrick always had.

He left the church through a side door and entered his favorite place, second only to the beach. Hidden from the public by tall green hedges, the garden reminded him of the book, The Secret Garden, which he'd read in school once. He'd pretended to scoff at the girly book, but secretly loved the description of that private world and its hidden mysteries.

Red, yellow and pink rose buds in various stages of opening lined the cobbled path, their sweet scent creating a natural perfume for the earth. The heat of the sun seemed to draw out even the most delicate of fragrances, which created a heady experience. He remembered playing in here as a child.

It had become his private sanctuary, just like the girl in the book. When he couldn't go to the beach, he'd come here. Father Patrick had fed and clothed him and kept him safe, even if that meant calling DSHS when a foster parent gave him a new broken bone or black eye. He would walk with Drake through the paths and tell him stories of Italy and the Pope and of his life before the Church.

When Father Patrick had to take confession, Drake would play hide and seek among the giant angel statues that stood watch over the roses. He would tell them his secrets and talk to them about the ocean. He knew Father Patrick had heard him sometimes, but the priest never interrupted or discussed what he'd heard. This garden had been his confessional, the angels his priests and guardians.

A scream broke Drake's reverie.

He rushed toward the sound, his heart pounding in his chest.

One of the large stone angels lay on its side, a young man pinned underneath. His screams filled the small courtyard.

Mrs. Maypol sat on the cobbled floor and held the boy's hand. She cried so hard her plump face matched the orange-red of her hair. "I'm so sorry. I'm so sorry."

Father Patrick stood a few feet away with a cell phone in his hand and a deep frown on his weathered face. Despite the fear that Drake knew the priest must have felt, Father Patrick stayed calm and commanding as he spoke to the 9-1-1 operator.

Drake assessed the situation. The young man's leg had been crushed by the angel. Blood spurted from what was likely a cut artery, spreading a crimson stain over the garden's path and into the soil. The roses would grow on the blood of this boy.

The ambulance wouldn't get there in time. The boy already looked a breath from death with his pale skin and glazed eyes.

Drake tore off his shirt and twisted it into a tourniquet, then handed it to Mrs. Maypol. "Keep him still! As soon as I lift the statue, immediately tie this around his leg above the injury. Make it tight."

She nodded, sweat pouring down her face from fear.

He looked into the terrified eyes of the trapped worker. The statue that pinned his leg probably weighed two thousand pounds. "Just hold on. I have to get this off you. When I do, the pain will be unbearable. Be ready."

The man didn't look ready for that at all, but Drake couldn't wait. He gripped the angel around the shoulder and pushed. Power flooded his veins and muscles. Superhuman strength flowed into him. His muscles bulged, his thighs stretched his jeans to near tearing, and his arms and torso turned rock hard. He pushed, willing the angel to fly.

And it did.

In a heartbeat, the statue stood on its base and the now-freed man screamed again and passed out.

Mrs. Maypol did her job, tying the shirt around the top of the boy's thigh. He'd likely lose his leg, but at least he would live.

The surge of power spent, Drake slumped against a bench and hung his head. He wasn't tired, exactly, just depleted.

The offending angel looked down on him, red dripping from her chest; a fallen angel stained with her victim's blood. Drake wanted to offer her a chance to confess, just as she had done for him so many times, but Father Patrick's voice interrupted his thoughts.

The priest looked between Drake and the boy and spoke rapidly into the cell phone. Sirens blared in the distance.

It took him a moment, but as the reality of his situation settled in, Drake realized he'd made a mistake. He'd just exposed himself to two people who didn't know about his powers, and at a time when he needed to be more careful than ever. No one could know about his strength.

He sought answers in the eyes of his priest who covered the phone with his hand and spoke quietly to Drake. "Go to my office and stay there until I get you. We'll figure out something to tell them."

Again, Drake couldn't help but admire the calm assurance Father Patrick radiated. It would have been easy to believe that everything could work out okay, but he'd long since stopped believing in happy endings. Still, he obeyed the priest in a way he never obeyed anyone else, and slipped back into the church moments before the medics crashed through the garden.

***

Drake paced the small office for so long he could have sworn there would be ruts in the hardwood floor.

He read every title on the bookshelves that lined the wall—mostly religious books, but, surprisingly, some fiction, and a few books on psychic powers and occult studies.

The small golden cross on the wall behind the desk looked recently polished and gleamed in the light. He felt no power from it, and had no attachment to a symbol that just represented death to him. Still, the cross had hung there longer than Drake had been coming to the church, and its familiarity offered a small comfort, albeit fleeting.

Despite every attempt to distract himself, his mind returned to what had just happened.

He worried about the man he'd saved. He worried about Father Patrick and Mrs. Maypol and what they'd say. And he worried about himself. Would Father Patrick be able to protect him, or would he finally be exposed to the world?

He rarely felt vulnerable. With the powers he controlled, he didn't know anyone who could pose a risk to him. So why didn't that reassure him this time?

A creak sounded from the hall.

The doorknob twisted.

Drake froze and waited, ready to attack if anyone but Father Patrick walked through that door.

The door opened.

"Relax, boy, it's just me. You're safe."

In that moment, Drake had to fight the urge to cry. *What the hell?* He never cried. Ever. He scowled instead, and then smoothed his face when he caught the old priest looking at him.

Father Patrick sat behind the desk and pointed Drake to the guest chair. "You saved that boy's life. The medics said if he'd been trapped any longer he would have been dead before they got here."

"What did you tell them?"

"That God saved the boy. It was a miracle. Mrs. Maypol backed me up. An angel came from the sky and moved the statue. They think we're crazy, and likely have no idea what to write in their report, but they're gone and no one knows you were involved."

Drake smirked. Leave it to Father Patrick to get away with that kind of story.

A weight lifted from Drake's shoulders—another possible exposure averted. "Where's Mrs. Maypol? What does she think about all of this?"

"She went to the hospital with Ralph. That's the young man you saved. He was helping us move some things around in the garden. I think she's suspected there's more to you for a long time, but she loves you and would never betray you. Don't worry about that."

"That's not what worries me. While surfing this morning, I had a sense that someone was watching me. Then I saw a man in black before he got in his car and drove away. I know it sounds paranoid, but you always said I should trust my instincts."

He also told the priest about his fight with Brad, and his best friend's concern about exposure with this contest.

Father Patrick stayed silent until the end. "What do you think you should do?"

Drake sighed. "I hate when you do that."

"When I make you think for yourself? Yes, I'm wretched that way."

"I want to stay in the competition. I can't live my life in hiding forever."

Father Patrick's kind eyes held Drake's for several long moments. "You're on a path none of us can understand. You have to do what's right for your heart. I can only tell you that I do see dark spirits around you, so whatever course you choose, be careful."

His words sent chills through Drake. Father Patrick's sixth sense was unparalleled. If he said Drake was in danger, Drake believed him, but that didn't mean dropping out of the competition would keep him safe.

Drake said goodbye to Father Patrick, and an unexpected melancholy swelled in his heart. He hugged the old man, who stood a good foot shorter than him.

"I'll come by tomorrow to help with the rest of the garden."

The priest pierced Drake with his eyes. "Be well, Son. Whatever happens, know that you have a destiny to fulfill in this world."

Strange parting words, but not unusual for someone who enjoyed the cryptic. Still, they unsettled Drake.

The feeling intensified as he walked out.

A horn beeped, and the shy girl who'd sold him tamales not so long ago hurried up to him with her cart, only her smile had turned to fear. "Señor, alguien que ha destrozado su coche."

"What? Who vandalized my car? What did you see?"

The force of his words frightened the timid girl. He calmed his voice. "I'm sorry to scare you. Please, tell me what happened."

He followed her around the corner to his car, which sat lower to the ground than it should, and... something had been painted on his windows.

"Shit!" He ran to the car, fearing what he'd find.

All four tires had been cut and the word "FREEK!"—misspelling and all—had been spray-painted across his window.

"Who did this? Did you see?"

Her eyes widened. "I sorry. I couldn't stop him. I scared of big man in black."

"It's okay. You did the right thing. It's not worth getting hurt over. Thank you for telling me."

The damage looked like some kids pulling a prank, but a big man in black sounded more like a hit posed to look like a prank. Why? To scare him?

Drake pulled out a twenty-dollar bill and handed it to the girl. "Thank you for telling me."

She nodded, slipped the money into her pocket, and dashed off.

Drake pulled his phone out and called Brad. "Dude, someone knows."

CHAPTER 4 – SAM

Music blared from Luke and Lucy's suite, next door to my own room. I let myself in and plopped down on their overstuffed purple couch.

Lucy saw me and turned down the radio. "What happened?"

I tossed her the file.

Luke walked through the wall from his bedroom into the living room and stood behind his sister to read. He frowned when he noticed the dates. "What about your interview, and the contest?"

"Higgins said he'd try to get me in, but I've got to take this assignment." I sighed and flopped back on the couch. "This totally sucks."

Lucy sat next to me with her arm draped over my shoulders. "At least you got your painting done. Come on, no more moping. It's Saturday. Let's eat junk food and watch movies."

So we did. All weekend long.

When Monday arrived, so bright and early, I had a major sugar hangover, but my mood had improved from sustained and prolonged contact with my cheer squad. I survived Calculus, barely, and Computer Programming, with Lucy's expert help—the hacker genius that she was— and a few other classes not worth mentioning, and finally made it to my favorite class. All of us had an advisor with whom we met once a week to practice our para-power skills. I had Mr. K.

His normally angst-ridden self seemed more angsty than normal today, if his all-black wardrobe and scowl were any indication. Still, my face lit up when he walked into the studio five minutes late.

He dropped his black leather satchel by his desk and sat down with a dramatic thud. "Sorry I'm late. It's been... a day."

"No problem. I'm just glad this is my last class until tomorrow."

He grunted and turned to pull out a sheet. "I'd hoped we could talk more about your painting and the art contest, but Higgins called me into his office and said I had to turn in an evaluation of you—immediately. That's why I'm late, if you care."

My heart skipped a beat. "Evaluations aren't due for months. Is everything all right?"

The vein above his eye popped out, and his fist clenched the paper as if it were something evil to be destroyed. "Is anything ever okay when it comes to this place?"

"Mr. K, why do you hate it here so much? Isn't this your dream job?"

The noise that came out of his throat didn't sound human. "More like nightmare. But I can't really talk about this, Sam. I'd get us both in trouble. And don't go probing my mind for secrets; you won't find anything helpful, just a few new expletives that a young lady such as yourself shouldn't use."

His glare challenged me to defy him, but I knew better. The few times I'd slipped into his mind uninvited hadn't ended well for either of us. I'd been in messy minds, tidy minds, perverse minds, but none as chaotic and terrifying as Mr. K's. Undoubtedly serial killers had worse minds, but they couldn't have been that much worse. Mr. K didn't just play the part of a dark and brooding artist; he'd created the part. His mind contained hidden corners that were best left to his mental cobwebs. There's a fine line between genius and madness, and while Mr. K was harmless, he wasn't entirely sane.

When I made no move to speak, he nodded and continued. "Today, you're going to draw what's in my mind, and, based on how well you do, I'll grade you for this ridiculous evaluation. Okay? Don't worry, I'll keep my mind calm for the assignment."

"Um, sure." His mind didn't frighten me when I had permission and stayed within the boundaries provided. This actually seemed a bit easy, but whatever. I reached for my bag to grab my supplies.

He put a hand up to stop me. "I have something for you."

He handed me a brown leather-bound sketchbook that looked well-used and smelled of old places and history. A round emblem, made of gold, was pinned to the cover. Its intricate shape reminded me of one of those meditation circles, but with a more elaborate design. The pages inside spoke to me in their own language, teasing me with drawings yet to be sketched. It even had a special compartment in the front for my pencils, and the paper looked like it could be refilled. I loved it immediately.

I pulled out the pencil already held there and opened the book up to the second page, saving the short dedication he'd written on the first page for a later read.

The chair underneath him squeaked as he pulled it forward so that we were uncomfortably close to each other. "Sam, it's important that you keep this sketchbook, and this sketch, safe. Do you understand?"

I nodded, though I didn't really understand his urgency, and poised my pencil to begin sketching.

He closed his eyes and I dipped into his mind. Humans don't think in linear thoughts, not usually. Most of the time people's minds are crowded with a blend of words, images, emotions, sensations and subconscious whispers. I spent a lot of years learning how to fill in the blanks and make sense of things in a way that would serve my work, so it wasn't difficult to push past the clutter in Mr. K's head to find the brightest image to draw. I just had to stay away from the dark corners, the places where his thoughts hadn't been tethered to the sane.

My hand raced furiously over the page, as if on autopilot. Time drifted into nothing and I became one with the art. Thirty minutes later Mr. K opened his eyes to examine my work.

"Remarkable. Sam, you've outgrown me in talent and ability. I'm so proud of the artist you've become."

I looked at the sketch in my hand and had to admit it rocked.

A wooden box, carved with the same symbol as the pin on my new sketchbook, and detailed images of nature took up the whole page. The box seemed to come alive, as if begging me to open it.

Mr. K smiled and made a few notes on his evaluation form.

I must have passed.

***

The next morning I waited by the front gate with Old Charlie and my very own bodyguard, who introduced himself as Gar. *What kind of name is Gar?*

Gar didn't talk much, but his rippled, veiny muscles, and a jaw so square it looked cartoonish, made him look scary—perfect for a bodyguard.

I clutched my overnight bag to my chest and shivered in the cool morning breeze. A limo arrived promptly at six and whisked me to the secret airstrip we used to fly to all of our assignments. The drive only took twenty minutes, and I never saw a highway or city sign, just trees and valleys of nothing.

Once there, Gar grabbed my overnight bag, but I strapped my backpack to my shoulders, not wanting to lose control of my most precious belongings. I boarded the Cessna Citation X, the world's fastest mid-sized jet, and sank into one of the plush leather seats.

I knew the drill: once we were airborne, Lollie, the stewardess, came to my seat with a needle balanced on a silver tray. I closed my eyes as she injected the drug into me, the one that would render me unconscious for the duration of my trip. This was for my protection, so I'd never be able to disclose the location of the Rent-A-Kid school. As always, it quelled any nervousness I had about the assignment.

My doubts and fears drifted away on a cloud, as darkness overcame me.

***

Something cool and soft tickled my forehead. My eyes pried themselves open as my head attempted to clear itself of the drug-induced fuzziness.

Lollie had her small hand pressed against my skin. "Time to wake up. We'll be at our destination in thirty minutes."

She handed me a cup of orange juice and a turkey sandwich and helped me get my seat into an upright position. The rush of sweet sugary fruit gave me clarity and a burst of energy. I tackled the sandwich like a man who hadn't eaten in a week—a common side effect of the drug.

With a few minutes to spare, I used the bathroom and brushed my teeth, then pulled my long brown hair into a bun. A quick touch-up to my lip gloss and a bit of mascara to accent my blue eyes, and I was ready to roll.

I went back to my seat and reviewed my file on the client one last time, though I knew the whole thing by heart. New last name, new identity. Each assignment we got a new name, but I didn't actually have a last name of my own. Didn't need one, really. The target had a son, Tommy. I hated assignments that involved kids, but what could I do? I pushed away my reservations and rehearsed my cover story in my head.

We landed at another private airstrip, where a middle-aged driver in a tux waited for us. "Sam Tinsley? Mr. Dollinger is waiting for you. Please come with me."

I climbed into the back and Gar sat in the front with the driver. The driver told us we were in Utah. This didn't register as anything terribly exciting for me. Once the limo hit the highway, I pulled out my new sketchbook and began drawing what I saw, which was mostly flatlands and farms, until we pulled into a wealthy neighborhood with big, lumbering mansions that looked out of place in their environment. Naturally, we beelined straight for the biggest, gaudiest one of them all.

A great cast iron gate with a lion's head crest blocked our entrance into the palatial estates. Gar took a moment to confirm with the guard, and, after a grating buzz and a few groans, the lion gate opened to allow us in. All around us, bushes trimmed into lion sentries stood guard as we passed. Someone had read too much C.S. Lewis.

My breath hitched in my throat when we arrived at the front door and a tall, lean man in a suit came out to greet us. He smiled at me through the tinted windows, but the smile looked painted on, like a clown's.

The driver opened the car door and I stepped out, straightened my spine and forced myself to meet my client's eyes.

He played his part well and held out his arms for me. Did he want a hug? Not happening. I shifted back, slightly, but enough to get my point across. His eyes flickered a flame of anger before he smothered it with false sincerity.

"You must be Sam. I haven't seen you since you were a baby, but your father says such great things about you. I'm sorry for everything you're going through, but rest assured, no harm will come to you while you're here."

Before I could reply, a small boy of about six ran out the front door with all the enthusiasm of youth. "Is she here? Is she here yet, Uncle Henry?"

"This must be Tommy." I raised an eyebrow. "Your nephew?"

He mussed the boy's hair while maintaining eye contact with me. "The Beaumont's son. We've been partners so long we're practically family."

I choked on his words. Right, family that's ready to throw each other under the bus for a buck. I shoved the judgment deep down and played my part in this farce—this family that wasn't a family—with as much enthusiasm as I could.

"Daddy says to say hi, and that he still remembers the night you drank too much and threw up on his date." I giggled like a rich, ditzy teenage girl and then smiled down at the boy, who hadn't stopped staring at me. For a moment, I let my real self come through. "Hi there. I'm Sam, what's your name?"

All boyish boldness fled as he dropped his big brown eyes and shyly muttered, "Tommy."

"Well, Tommy, did you know that I can draw any animal you can think of? Even animals that don't exist?"

His cherub face lit up in the happiest smile I'd ever seen, and I instantly fell in love with the little kid. A pang of guilt hit my heart.

Tommy belonged to the Beaumonts — the family I had been hired to ruin.

CHAPTER 5 – DRAKE

At four in the morning, Drake woke and couldn't fall back asleep. He hadn't told Father Patrick about his car or reported it to the police. Brad had given him enough grief as it was.

He rose, made coffee and sat on their balcony that overlooked the beach. His cell phone beeped — another text from Kylie asking if he planned to come over before the competition. His annoyance mounted, and he turned off the phone and ignored it.

The sun hadn't found its way to the coast yet, so Drake waited for sunrise in silence.

The crashing waves and smell of saltwater tried to calm him, but this time they failed. Despite his still body, his mind hammered out worry after worry. Brad had made him swear he'd at least consider dropping the competition, but Drake knew he wouldn't. He refused to run away from his dreams because of a few slashed tires and a bad feeling.

Oranges, reds and purples filled the dark sky as the sun reflected against the ocean's waves. He waited for the sun like a man waiting for a lover to come home. When the bright morning rays reached the balcony, he closed his eyes, basked in the warmth, and let all worry go for just a moment.

Brad's voice broke the spell. "You're going through with it, aren't you?"

Drake nodded.

"Come on, then, I'll walk with you."

They left for Venice Beach, where hordes of people would be gathered to see the competition—winning would earn him a place in the U.S. Open in Hawaii.

This had been Drake's dream since childhood. Each time he landed in a new foster home, he prayed it would be near the ocean. When it wasn't, he'd take busses for hours to get to the beach. Nothing could keep him away then, and nothing would keep him away now.

They arrived early enough that a large crowd hadn't yet formed. Drake found a spot for their boards and supplies, then put his wetsuit on, removed his surfboard from its bag, and rubbed it down with surf wax. The exotic coconut scent tickled his nose.

Soft arms wrapped themselves around his waist. He turned to face Kylie, and frowned.

She'd been a fling that had become too clingy. He didn't have time for, or interest in, a girlfriend—something he'd told her repeatedly—but Kylie didn't seem to get the message.

"Drakey, you didn't come over last night."

He backed up and placed his board between them. "What do you want, Kylie?"

"I'm your cheer squad, and I missed you. You never come by or hang out anymore. I just thought maybe you could use a little fun before you hit the waves. We could head to the bathrooms for some privacy."

He cringed in disgust. "Look, I had a good time with you, but, like I said before, I'm not looking for a relationship."

She puckered and pouted and puffed out her chest. "But we're so good together."

"No, we're really not. Go find someone else to drape yourself on. I'm not the guy for you."

He waited for her to leave, but her eyes turned to slits and she crossed her arms over her ample chest. "You can't get rid of me so easily, Drake. I'm not going anywhere. We belong together and I'm not leaving until you see that."

Seriously? His temper flared to life but he pushed it down. "Get out of here, Kylie. I mean it."

She reached for him and pushed herself against his chest. "Don't you want to at least say goodbye properly?"

A war raged in Drake. He couldn't use force on her; he didn't want to hurt her or attract attention.

The murmur of voices around him faded into the background and his focus zeroed in on her vacuous mind. In a voice anyone else would have had to strain to hear, he pushed all his power at her. "Go away, Kylie, and leave me alone. We're done."

He hadn't just nudged her this time, he'd put the full force of his power behind the compulsion.

She nodded, a vacant expression on her face, and walked away without another word.

A small twinge of guilt plagued him, but he ignored it easily enough. She'd be fine, and would soon enough latch on to another hot guy like the barnacle she was.

Brad arrived with two bottles of water. "What's up with Kylie?"

"Nothing. She won't be coming around anymore."

Brad shrugged but didn't say anything, and Drake appreciated the silence. He needed to get into the zone and prepare for the competition.

He'd never suffered from excessive paranoia, but as he drank his water, he couldn't shake the feeling that he was being followed... and not by a sponsor.

***

Max McKerry, the celeb surfer, broke the silence when he knocked into Drake's board. "You think you're going to beat me with that piece of shit? Dream on, loser."

Brad rolled his eyes at Drake but directed his comment to Max. "Get a life, man. Do you really think anyone here is scared of you?"

The cocky smile plastered on Max's face didn't fade in the least. "It doesn't matter. Your friend's going to lose either way. No way a homeless orphan is going to win this competition."

Words had no power over Drake. The insults slid off his back like water off a duck. One thought and Max's ass would be groveling on the hot sand begging to kiss Drake's toes, but that's not how he wanted to win, so he ignored the jerk and stayed in his zone.

He didn't get off on the competition against others; the real journey existed only between him and the ocean. Her power claimed him, and nothing else mattered. The glory, the sponsors, the trophies — they were only a means to an end, a way to live well, to have financial security while doing what he loved.

Max may have had a better surfboard and more fans, but he didn't know this water like Drake.

Brad grumbled and set up his chair in the sand. "I don't know why you don't put that guy in his place. He's a jackass."

"No point. He'll find his place when we're in the water. I'm not worried about it."

Drake's confidence was not misplaced or unfounded. As the day progressed, each set brought him closer to victory as other surfers were weeded out.

Finally, three surfers remained: he, Max, and a girl named Chrysta who had surprised them all with her entry and success. The surf crashed to the beach and pulled Drake into the open arms of the Pacific. He let everything go and emptied his mind of all worries, angers and fears. Floating and bobbing in the swells of water set his mind at ease. Thoughts floated in and out like the currents, but he paid them no mind; he only waited for the right wave.

Then it came, and all his focus went into paddling. Every muscle, every ounce of energy, pushed him toward the pulsing water. In that last moment, he stood and glided on top of the wave, slicing through the surf.

Eckharte Tolle wrote in *The Power of Now*, "If the primary focus of your life is the now, then you will be free from pain and suffering." Drake understood those words only when surfing. In that moment, nothing else mattered, and no other thoughts or feelings had any chance to hatch and take hold. In that moment, only the wave mattered.

In a perfect moment of synchronicity and connection, the wave broke and wrapped him in a watery cocoon from which he would emerge reborn. In that state of bliss, he barely noticed Max cutting him off, barely felt the pull of the current until his board threatened to spill him into the depths of the ocean.

With paranormal strength, he steadied himself and kept his feet under him. A look of surprise flashed across Max's face before he directed his attention to the wave that also threatened to engulf him.

The men rode their boards to shore and were greeted by hundreds of voices cheering their success.

To anyone watching, they had both just scored a serious victory. Even the judges wouldn't be able to tell that Max had cheated and tried to sabotage Drake.

Words mattered little to him, but Max had just declared war.

Drake shoved Max to the sand using a touch more than normal strength, just enough to sting. "What the hell, man? Are you so desperate to win, and so afraid of me, that you would cheat?"

Max's eyes turned cold, but he pushed himself up and stared at Drake. "I don't know what you're talking about, but do that again and I'll make sure you're disqualified from the final round."

A group had formed, drawn into the drama. Drake passed his board to Brad and stormed off toward the showers to cool down before he blew it for good.

***

The warm sand squished under his feet, and the hot sun blazed down on his head.

He stripped off his wetsuit and stood under the showers, letting the warm water wash away the sand, salt and anger. Today could change his life forever; he just needed to keep his cool and ignore Max.

He'd been so absorbed in his rage that he hadn't noticed the buzz of warning under his skin that someone was watching him.

By the time he felt it, it was too late.

Something stung his shoulder.

He reached around and pulled out a dart. His thoughts swirled around in his head, and his recent clarity gave way to a jumble of incoherent ramblings.

"Dude, are you all right?"

A voice spoke to him, but male or female, he couldn't tell. His vision blurred and he slumped onto the wet cement, the now cold water spraying over him until it ran out of time and stopped.

"Drake, you'll be okay. Come on, boy." Another voice he didn't recognize.

He reached out with his mind to stop whoever was touching him, but nothing happened. His power didn't work. Then he felt it, the compulsion to obey, directed at him as someone siphoned his powers from him.

When hands pulled him away from the familiar noises, he tried to fight with his muscle.

"Damn it, he's still too strong. Get him to the van, quick."

"Don't worry," one voice said to the other. "Drake, you will relax and walk quietly to the van with us. You will not put up a fight or make any noise."

Drake nodded, stood and walked forward.

Before he could process anything more, a painful whack to his head sent him tumbling toward darkness.

The leader yelled at whoever had hit him, and then Drake found that darkness.

CHAPTER 6 – SAM

The next morning, I still had nothing on Beaumont, but my bond with Tommy had deepened, not in small part to the twenty new drawings I'd given him of the most fantastical creatures he could think of.

The kid had quite an imagination.

He followed me everywhere, and I didn't mind. Between him and my Gar shadow, I had a freaking entourage. A longing for a real family with a little brother just like Tommy threatened to undo me, but I smacked it down and stayed focused on my work. Mostly.

It would have helped if Mr. Beaumont had actually been home more. My mind reading skills weren't all-powerful. I required some proximity to my target if I wanted to connect with him, especially someone with an unfamiliar mental signature. It was like a voice in the crowd—the more familiar the voice, the easier it was to pinpoint and lock onto it.

That morning I finally had my chance to corner Dollinger without Tommy tagging along. The pressure to finish up this assignment so I could leave the next day weighed heavy in my mind, and pushed me into confrontations I would normally have avoided.

I found my client pouring himself a stiff drink in the study, and got straight to the point. "I can't do what you hired me for without access to the target. When will Mr. Beaumont be home?"

His eyes hardened into black coal, but he kept his tone civil. "He's going to surprise everyone with a trip to the fair today. You'll have an all-day pass to his mind. Use it well."

'For what I'm paying her, she'd better find the mother lode of dirt on this bastard.... I'm sick of being his lackey.'

I shook his thoughts out of my head and left the room.

Tommy squealed and threw himself into my arms. "Sam, Daddy's home. And guess what? He's taking us all to the fair! Isn't that great?"

'This is going to be the best day ever.... Maybe Sam can live with us forever and be my big sister.... I can't wait to eat cotton candy.... Daddy's the best.'

My heart cracked. I gave serious thought to dropping this whole thing and telling Higgins I couldn't get anything from the target. Then, I wouldn't have to destroy Tommy's life, and the guilt that ate me alive would go away.

But I would have to stay at least two weeks before pulling an assignment. Rules. If I did that, I'd miss my interview and my contest, and when they released me from Rent-A-Kid in three months I'd have nothing.

How could I seriously consider destroying Tommy's life so I could get into a decent college? His brown eyes and innocent thoughts crashed into me. With a sinking in my gut, I knew what I had to do — blow the assignment, regardless of the cost to me.

I mentally waved farewell to all of my dreams as I took Tommy's hand and helped him get ready for the fair.

***

Utah millionaires weren't uncommon, it appeared, but it didn't change the charm of small town fairs. In a large field, a spectacle of lights and sounds had been erected to entertain the populace. Colorful booths attracted kids of all ages to win cheap toys and stuffed animals by throwing balls in cups or shooting down fake bunny targets. A large carrousel stood in the center of the fair, an iconic symbol of the American heartland.

Tommy only cared about one thing: cotton candy. He darted through throngs of people to snag his place in a long line of sugar-craving children.

Mrs. Beaumont hadn't joined us, as she was attending some event or another for her social club. Mr. Dollinger had begged out by claiming work duties, then eyed me with a look that meant I'd better come home with something good to tell him.

I had no intention of doing any such thing, but his absence did make for an awkward dynamic with the three of us, plus my Gar shadow, who just stood and watched and never said a word. While Tommy's dad presented a respectable and attractive front, something about him made my skin crawl. Yet he'd been incredibly generous, hospitable and kind since my arrival — at least when he was actually present.

Though I had decided not to pursue the assignment, I couldn't help dipping into his thoughts from time to time. Money and work consumed his mental focus. He didn't give much airtime to family or anything else, really, which sucked for Tommy but wasn't a crime. It did strike me as odd that he'd taken us all to the fair today, though. He wasn't the kind of man who enjoyed spending the day with his son, while they ate sugary treats together.

We inched up in line, and Mr. Beaumont pulled out $200 and handed it to me. "Sam, would you mind taking care of Tommy for a bit? I need to find a bathroom and make a call. Just get him whatever he wants and take him on some rides."

Tommy's face fell when he realized his dad planned to ditch us.

I covered my anger with a smile and took the money. "Sure. Will you be joining us later?"

His eyes glazed over and he didn't make eye contact, distracted by something else. "I'll catch up with you two in a bit."

And in that moment, I became the world's most expensive babysitter... on his partner's dime. Rent-A-Kid charged at least $150,000 a day for my time. That worked out to $6,250 per hour if you count sleep. I didn't see all that money, obviously, but still... I had to laugh at the absurdity of it. I would've felt worse for Mr. Dollinger if he weren't such a jerk. The only person I cared about in all of this was Tommy, and so I would do my best to protect him.

To that end, I slipped into his father's mind as I paid for Tommy's pink- and blue-swirled sugar high.

'Too bad Tommy's a boy... girl would have been better... easier to... ah yes... nice fresh meat... mustn't touch... just look... until later... later I can touch that innocent flesh... when no one is around... tomorrow night... they promised me a young one, I can't wait to —'

Enough! My stomach clenched and bile rose in my throat. The air around me thickened until it became hard to breathe. My world narrowed to a pinpoint, as though I would pass out at any moment. I couldn't just hear his thoughts; I could see the images playing around in his mind. In that moment I wanted to gouge out my third eye.

Large hands held me upright and tiny hands tugged at my sweater. "Sam! Sam! Are you okay? What's wrong, Sam?"

My vision focused on Tommy's big eyes widened in fear. Gar stood behind me to keep me from falling.

I composed myself and found the ground under my feet. "I'm okay. I just got dizzy for a second. Probably just need to eat something."

Tommy nodded as if all of life's problems could be solved with food. He pulled me toward the food court. "Come on, we'll get you a hotdog. They are the best ever!"

Gar stood just inches from me with a look that I could have mistaken as concern, if I thought he cared at all. "Are you okay? Did you get something on the father?"

I didn't try to hide my surprise. He hadn't expressed any interest in my assignment until that moment, but it helped to have him on my side.

I nodded. "It's bad. Can I use your phone?"

He narrowed his eyes but pulled it out of his jacket pocket. "Who are you calling?"

"Dollinger."

I dialed the number from memory and tapped my foot as it rang. "Keep an eye on Tommy, okay?"

Gar's face squished together as though I'd asked him to change a dirty diaper, but he moved his eyes to Tommy, who was busy eating his treat—at least that part of it not smeared across his face.

My client's voice came on the line. "This is Sam. I have what you need to take down Beaumont." I told him what I'd overheard in the man's mind.

I hated to hurt Tommy this way, but leaving him in the care of that monster would have been worse.

Once I filled Dollinger in on the details, I expected him to say that I had done my job and was free to go.

"That's not enough. We need hard proof. Keep digging."

"What? You need to stop him before tomorrow night. Before he...." I couldn't even bring myself to finish the sentence.

"This isn't about stopping him. It's about catching him red-handed so he can't weasel out of this with his fancy lawyers and destroy everything I've worked for."

I couldn't decide who was the bigger monster, but in that moment I wanted them both to pay.

I handed the phone back to Gar, and forced myself to keep up with Tommy the rest of the day.

After several rides and more junk food, I just couldn't focus.

Tommy could tell that my mind was elsewhere. "Sam, what's wrong? Are you still sick? Do you want a nap?"

"I'm okay, but it's probably time we find your dad and head home. Your mom will want to hear about the exciting day you've had."

His blue, candy-covered lips frowned, but he didn't argue.

I pretended to look for Mr. Beaumont, even though I knew exactly where he was.

We found him by the merry-go-round, which Tommy insisted on riding.

Mr. Beaumont stood a little too close to me as we watched his son balance on the horse. His dark blue three-piece suit, nice tan, and fit physique hid the monster lurking beneath the pretty veneer. From his perfectly highlighted caramel hair to his glow-in-the-dark teeth, he screamed "fake." I imagined his skin peeling off to reveal a slimy troll, complete with red beady eyes and swollen pink lips oozing something green.

What did the little girls see when he first walked in to greet them? Did they see a respectable man in his early 40s, someone safe and nice? Or could they sense the impending danger?

He smiled at me as if he knew what I was thinking. "Sam, have you enjoyed the fair?"

"Yes, but I'm not feeling well. I think I ate something that didn't agree with me."

He checked his phone. "We'll be leaving after this ride. I have to get to work."

The whole ride home, I fought an internal war. Should I listen to his thoughts or not? I couldn't stomach hearing more of his vile intentions, but if Dollinger wasn't satisfied, more information would help.

I slipped back in, but he had put aside his perversions for worry over work.

I would have to find another way to catch this bastard.

CHAPTER 7 – SAM

For a man who'd hardly been home the last two days, Mr. Beaumont sure broke his pattern that afternoon. He locked himself in his home office, the one place I needed to be to get Dollinger what he wanted.

Nothing revolted me more than spending time in his mind, but I had to maintain mental contact to complete this mission.

After a long evening and a sleepless night tossing and turning in the guest room, I finally got my chance to snoop the next morning when my target left for work.

While Tommy spent some time with his mother, I snuck into Mr. Beaumont's office and locked it behind me. Gar joined me, as I didn't want him standing guard outside—might as well put up flashing neon lights announcing my intentions, in that case.

Gar stood by the door and watched as I turned on Mr. Beaumont's desktop computer. I'd seen him use his phone and iPad to check appointments, and he probably had a backup calendar on his computer. I'd already captured his password from my long—and torturous—evening of mental spying.

Lucy could have just hacked into his system without the mind probes, but I had to rely on old-fashioned methods.

A few clicks of the keys and up popped his calendar.

My heart raced as I scanned his daily appointments, looking for anything that might incriminate him, while simultaneously scanning the house mentally to make sure I wouldn't get caught.

Work. Work. Business appointment. Work.

Nothing jumped out at me. I looked for anything that evening, as his thoughts had indicated some kind of rendezvous with a young girl.

He'd listed a phone number next to 7 p.m. I jotted it down in a notebook, then pulled open his browser history and looked through his desktop files. I'd need more than a random number to get him.

My hands shook and my stomach heaved at the images I found. The idiot had even photographed himself with young girls. I copied it all onto my USB drive and shut down the computer as quickly as possible. I needed to get out of this house and back to school.

My sweaty palm slipped on the doorknob just as my mind latched onto Mr. Beaumont's. He was home and heading my way. Panic scissored through me. I hid the USB and looked to Gar for guidance, but what could he do? I'd gotten us into this and I'd have to get us out.

Mr. Beaumont would see me leaving his office, but I had to risk it. With a fake smile so big it hurt my cheeks, I walked out and ran straight into his chest. My skin crawled at the contact with this psycho.

"Sam, what are you doing in my office?"

"Looking for you, of course. But you weren't there. I was wondering if you wanted to try another afternoon at the fair? I'm feeling better and thought it might be fun."

Please say no. Please say no.

"I'm sorry, Sam, but I've got some work to do, and I'll be gone this evening for meetings." He pulled out another $300 from his wallet. "If you want to take Tommy, you two have fun. It's on me."

I pocketed the money and slunk away, fighting the vomit that rose in my throat.

I walked into the family room and found Tommy, wearing pressed jeans and a salmon-colored polo shirt, playing on the floor with his yellow truck.

"Vroom, vroom. Watch this, Sam." He crashed the truck into the leg of a handmade rosewood table. Probably not something Tommy should bang against. The whole room could have been modeled after a magazine spread. Not exactly kid friendly with the $3,000 knickknacks. Who spent that much on a decorative egg?

The clicking of high heels—Manolo Blahnik, naturally, because Prada was so last season—approached from behind. Mrs. Beaumont pranced in, tall, blonde and elegant, with big brown eyes like Tommy, draped in a cream cashmere dress that hugged her curves. My jeans and t-shirt just couldn't compete.

"Tommy dear, no slamming toys into the furniture. Why don't you go in your room and play?"

"But Sam is here. I want to play with Sam."

"Actually," I said, "I'm looking for Mr. Dollinger. Have either of you seen him?"

According to her husband's thoughts, she was a dead fish in bed and therefore the cause of his perversions. Yeah, right.

She looked relieved that my presence would no longer be an argument point for the boy. "Yes, he's on his cell phone by the pool. At least he was a moment ago."

I thanked her, gave Tommy a quick hug, and excused myself to the backyard. Gar trailed behind me.

***

This level of wealth didn't impress me the way it might some. We lived well at Rent-A-Kid, with the best of everything—I'd endured so many formal dinners, etiquette training, and socialization classes. At least we enjoyed everything money could buy. After all, we had to impress and fit in with some of the wealthiest people in the world.

Still, their custom pool looked more fitting for a resort than a backyard, with slides in different sizes and shapes, and rock formations and plant life strategically placed to give the whole space a tropical feel. A few fruity drinks with umbrellas, and you'd never know you were in Utah.

Under a transplanted palm tree, my client engaged in an urgent conversation with someone in hushed tones. His pressed pinstripe suit hardly fit the pool setting.

Hmmm... wonder what has money bags so riled?

When he saw me, he ended the conversation and slipped his iPhone into his pocket.

"What is it, Sam?" *'I really hope she's not reading my mind right now... how can I get her to stop?... lalalala... I hope this plan works and I get rid of this ass... does my wife know about Lisa?... it only happened once... no need to tell her... am I getting fat?... maybe I should hit the gym harder when this is all over... Sam is hot... I wonder... such long silky brown hair... clear skin... bright blue eyes... no... she's just a kid... shit... is she listening to me?'*

"He has kiddie porn on his computer." I handed him a slip of paper. "Here's a number for his mystery meeting tonight at 7 p.m. You should have everything you need to put him away for good and take over his business."

He smiled, but it didn't reach his eyes. His smiles never did. "This is great news. Thanks, I'll call and let them know you did well."

I turned to walk away.

His thoughts stopped me. *'How best to play this... what should I do...? could use this information to my advantage.'*

Did I really want to get involved? I'd completed my job. Time to return to Rent-A-Kid. Just walk away. The aftereffects of my work were irrelevant. Not my problem.

I couldn't move. My traitorous body refused to follow my mental commands to keep walking. My heart beat so rapidly I thought it would leap right out of my chest.

I turned to face him, questioning my own sanity even as I did. "You are going to stop him from hurting that girl, aren't you?"

"Yes, of course, I'm as outraged as you. Honestly, I had no idea he had this kind of secret. I assumed we'd catch him at something more benign, like money laundering or tax evasion." *'Disgusting bastard... no idea he was so foul... still... if I get video and pictures... catch him red-handed... I can blackmail him forever... better than just getting him arrested... right?... more money and control for me... could hire someone....'*

"No!" My outburst surprised even me. "You can't let him hurt that girl and get away to do it again to someone else. You have to stop him."

"Look, kid, you stay out of my head. I didn't pay you to spy on my thoughts, you hear me?"

The threat of danger bit at me, warning me. Years of unquestioning obedience transformed into a new, entirely unexpected rebellion.

I recalled Beaumont's thoughts. His plans. His past deeds. "I really don't care about your money. I do care about that little girl and all the other little girls he might hurt. So you are going to make sure he is arrested and found guilty, or your wife will get a mysterious note exposing your secret with Lisa."

I reflected on my perfect track record, my future at Sarah Lawrence College, the art contest, the consequences to those who had broken the rules. Would I be fined? Forced to clean the bathrooms with a toothbrush? I weighed all this in my mind, knowing the answer instantly. I knew too much, had seen and heard too much.

No matter. I no longer cared what happened to me.

His face turned bright red, hands balled into fists, jaw grinding.

Might as well add some fuel to the growing fire. "And you should definitely consider hitting the gym. You're getting love handles, and your wife isn't finding them too sexy."

His hand flew at me, and the pain exploded in my cheek as I crashed into the pool. Darkness drew me close, surrounding me in a watery cocoon. Awareness flittered into oblivion. The pain receded into a dull background noise easily tuned out. I barely felt the strong arms pull me out and lay me unceremoniously on the warm tile.

Gar helped me to stand. Dizziness sent me into the arms of my silent sentry.

He held onto me as I regained my balance, then turned to Dollinger with a fierce expression on his face. "That was a mistake." Gar lifted our client by the collar. "Apologize."

I tried to focus my sights on our client, but something blocked my vision. I swiped at my face, and flinched. It felt like a giant golf ball had taken up residence in my eye socket. "Gar, it's okay. Put him down."

Gar paused for a moment, and just when I thought he would beat the man bloody, he dropped him onto the cement.

I did my best to lock eyes with Dollinger. I'd never been physically abused before, and my whole body shook from the pain, adrenaline, and fear. "You will never touch me again. And you will make sure this pervert is put away for good. If you don't, I'll make your life hell. I can reach you anywhere, find out anything about you, and destroy you. Are we clear?"

He glared at me, then at my muscleman, and nodded.

I walked back to the house with the help of my guard.

***

"Oh my dear, what happened? Are you okay?" Mrs. Beaumont rushed to me, her concern masked by too many Botox injections.

"I'm fine, I think. I slipped and fell in the pool. Must've hit my head on the side."

"Come on, dear, let's dry you off and get ice on that. Perhaps we should take you to the doctor."

"No, no doctors. I just need to lie down."

After a warm shower and dry clothes, I rested on my guest bed with ice packs that Tommy replaced each time they melted.

"You're a good nurse, kid."

His eyes glowed bright at the compliment as he eased a fresh icepack onto my face. "You didn't fall,

Sam," he whispered. "I saw Uncle Henry hit you. Why would he hurt you like that? That's not right."

I sat up to face him. "I'm sorry you had to see that, buddy. You're right, he shouldn't have done that. But I need you to do me a favor."

"What, Sam?"

"I need you to keep this just between us. No one else can know, okay?"

My heart constricted at his confusion and sadness. How could I do this to him? How could I ask him to lie, to cover up abuse, when I'd just jeopardized my assignment to expose his father? But what choice did I have? I couldn't risk any more problems. I shuddered at the thought of my potential punishments for what I'd already done.

"You want me to lie?"

"Oh, Tommy, I don't know. Of course I don't want you to lie. But there's more going on here than I can tell you right now. Do you trust me?"

"Yes, I sure do!"

"Then please don't tell anyone, okay? And remember, no matter what happens after I leave, I love you and have done everything I can to protect you."

He nodded and snuggled into the bed with me.

I relished those few moments of innocence before I got up to prepare to leave.

By that evening, both my eyes were nearly swollen shut. Gar made the arrangements and scheduled a pickup for me, but I had one more thing to do before we left.

I found Mrs. Beaumont in the kitchen. "Do you have a computer I can borrow? I just want to email my friends that I'm coming home."

"Of course, dear. We're sad to see you go, but so happy that you're no longer in danger."

They had bought the cover story, and now that my assignment was complete, my "father" no longer needed me ensconced in safety.

She led me to her study and logged me into her computer. "There you go. Take your time, I'll be in the living room if you need any help."

"Thank you." Guilt prodded me to talk more than I should have. "Mrs. Beaumont, if something were to happen to your husband, would you and Tommy be okay?"

Her face probably couldn't register surprise, what with the Botox, but a small tear formed in the corner of her eye. "Don't you worry about us, Sam. I know more than you think, and I'll always make sure Tommy is taken care of."

She left the room and left me with more questions than answers. Did she know about her husband's extracurricular activities?

I slipped the memory stick into the computer and opened up an email as Mrs. Beaumont. It only took a second to find the FBI email address for tips. I attached the pictures, wrote a brief message exposing Mr. Beaumont, and hit Send. Right or wrong, I had to be sure this bastard paid.

Gar had stood behind me the whole time, probably to make sure I didn't expose Rent-A-Kid in any way. When I looked at him, he gave a curt nod. I think he approved of my choice.

He checked his watch. "We have to go now."

Before we left the room, I pulled Gar around to face me. "Thank you for defending me, and for letting me do this."

His lips twitched just the slightest. "I have a daughter. You did the right thing."

He turned and walked away before I could say anything else. I tried to imagine Gar with a family, but the picture didn't fit—like that "which of these doesn't belong" game. But everyone had to come from somewhere. No one was created in a lab.

Gar had left the door open for me, and I went back to the guest room to get my bags and make sure I hadn't forgotten anything.

Time to say goodbye to Tommy.

He clung to me and cried, begging me not to leave.

In a move that broke more rules than I could count, I slipped a picture into his pocket of the two of us, from the fair we'd gone to. I'd managed to get pictures of us together in one of those booths while Gar used the bathroom. Don't leave any evidence of your presence. Avoid cameras and photos. Remove surveillance before you leave. Erase anything with your image on it. They'd drilled those rules into me since I was a kid. But I gave Tommy something no one in the outside world had: a tangible reminder that I'd been there.

"I don't want you to go. Can't you stay? Please? I promise I'll be good!" He looked at me with those big sad eyes.

I fought back the tears. "No matter what, remember that I love you. If you ever get scared, just close your eyes and meet me in that special room we made together in our minds. Remember?"

"Yes, Sam, I remember." His voice cracked on my name. Tears slid down his soft, baby cheeks.

"I'll always be able to hear you, and you'll know I'm there, okay?" I hoped. Having memorized his mental frequency, I planned to check up on him, if I could reach that far. Maybe once out on my own, I could find a way to help him. Distance reading was no simple task, but I would get better. I had to.

I kissed him on the cheek and plopped into the limo, slinging my book bag onto the seat next to me. My guard sat in the front with the driver.

A phone rang. I answered it, knowing who it was ahead of time.

"You broke protocol." Higgins didn't sound happy.

"Yes, I had to," I replied without remorse.

"You'd better hope this doesn't get out of our control, Sam. Otherwise, your retirement plans might be affected."

The threat lingered like the monster of long ago, hiding in my closet at night, waiting for me to fall asleep. Whatever. I didn't regret my choices.

"Everything will be fine," I said. And I believed it.

CHAPTER 8 – DRAKE

When Drake regained some semblance of consciousness, intense pain stripped every nerve ending raw. His mind felt crushed into his skull, not just from the hit to the head—his powers gave him the ability to heal faster than most—but from the mind assault when someone used Drake's powers against him. How was that even possible?

He didn't open his eyes. First, he wanted to get a sense of his environment. Wheels clanked against a linoleum floor and he felt himself move forward. Voices floated around him like clouds. The world around him drifted through his awareness like bubbles—so fragile and immaterial.

He'd been drugged. He remembered the dart to his arm, but he suspected they'd given him something more since taking him.

Who did this? Where was he?

Questions swirled through his mind, and he couldn't steady his thoughts enough to make sense of anything.

He had clothes on, not just his bathing suit, so someone had dressed him. The air smelled of chemicals and sickness, like a hospital.

Darkness threatened to close in on him again. Panic filled his veins and sent a small shot of adrenaline through him.

Another mind connected with his—someone with similar powers, someone who could help. He reached out, pushing his mind with the little strength he had left.

He squinted through pain, and locked eyes with a dark-haired, pale-faced beauty who looked as if she'd been in a bar fight. One blue eye shined bright with intelligence, while the other was swollen nearly shut. Her pink lips curved into a frown, and she placed a fist on the swell of her hips, which accented her petite frame.

A protective instinct flared and Drake wanted to defend her against whoever had given her that black eye, but he couldn't be the knight when he needed saving himself.

He reached out to her mind. *'Help me.'*

She held his fate in her mind. Before he collapsed back into oblivion he willed her to help, willed her to remember him and find a way to free him.

As he sank into nothing, her blue eyes, fair face and dark hair haunted him, and he was left with one thought: she's mine.

CHAPTER 9 – SAM

No matter how many times I'd been drugged, I still woke up in a slight panic. My body maintained no sense of how long it had been. My subconscious mind had been shut out—definitely the worst part of any assignment.

Wait....

Mary lay in the bed next to mine. That sucked worse.

She sneered at me from behind her blond hair. "Well, look who finally woke up. Took you long enough. Had some trouble, huh? Is Higgins's pet turning rebel?"

"What do you want, Mary?" Though sick of her games, ignoring her would only inspire her to greater taunts.

"Nothing. Just waiting on the good doctor, like you."

I slipped into her mind, like being stuck in the poisonous trap of a viper. *'Thinks she's so great... not that great... not even as pretty as everyone thinks... tits too small... and look at that black eye... looks like she finally screwed up... hope she gets what's coming to her... she's just a goody two-shoes... little priss.'*

Well, nothing new there. Did she ever have any other kind of thought?

I raised myself on the bed. The world spun just a little through my swollen eyes. Fake flowers in artificially bright colors stood on the table by the window, a futile attempt to cheer up the dreary grey walls and fluorescently lit room.

The tiny Dr. Sato walked into the room. "Ah, Sam, Mary, you both wake. Good," she said with a soft voice.

Why is she nervous?

Her pronounced Japanese accent, stronger than usual, gave away her unease. "How you feeling?"

I stretched my arms and moved my neck around to work out the kinks. The inside of my mouth reeked. "Fine, just a bit of a headache." Probably brought on by my roommate. Well, and the black eye.

"And you, Mary?" she asked.

"I feel wonderful." Mary crossed her long legs seductively and purred. Her slinky silver gown showed off more than it covered. Who the hell was she trying to impress in here? Her para-power to seduce couldn't claim any new victims in the absence of heterosexual men.

Dr. Sato took my blood pressure, checked my temperature, and examined my eyes and cheek. "You bruised. Bone hurts, but you be better soon. Just no jumping."

Again with the nervousness.

I slipped into her mind but met only gibberish, having never had a chance to learn her particular dialect. It unnerved me—nothing clear, as if I'd lost my hearing or eyesight. Normally, the images that filled her mind were of her homeland or the clinic, benign and useless to me.

Today I felt terror coming off her, and saw a flash of a man with a gold tooth leaning over an unconscious girl.

"You go now. Headmaster Higgins expects you. You get dizzy or have troubles with eye, come back. And you take it easy until eye sees better. And no jumping too. Okay?"

I nodded and bit back a comment about how hard it would be to refrain from jumping everywhere.

My book bag sat on the chair by the fake flowers. I hopped off the bed—*oops, does that count as a jump?*—grabbed it, and walked through the long corridors to the exit while processing Dr. Sato's dark thoughts. Confronting Higgins always made my stomach hurt, but getting away from Mary made it worth it.

Few people walked the corridors of the clinic. Where were all the normal personnel?

I stopped at the front desk to sign out. *Something's out of place.*

A movement caught the corner of my eye.

A boy, about my age, tall and muscular, lay unconscious on a stretcher. I only saw a glimpse through the electric doors to the surgery. His messy blonde hair had flecks of red in it. Dried blood. A gash ran over his forehead. As the doors closed, his eyes flashed open and held mine for one long moment.

'Help me.'

The mental message sent me staggering back in its ferocity. An urgent compulsion to respond overwhelmed me, a need to do as he'd asked.

Then the boy lost consciousness. My mind cleared, and whatever had grabbed hold of me disappeared.

Missy, an attractive, plump woman who worked the front desk, frowned. "Are you okay? Should I call the doctor?"

"No, I'm fine. I just... head's still hurting, you know."

She did know. Her eyes gleamed with sympathy. I'd always liked her. She baked us cookies from time to time, and kept her blond hair in a messy bun held together with random pencils. I'd tried it once on my hair, but couldn't make it stay put.

"Missy, who was that boy they were wheeling in? He looked hurt, but I don't recognize him."

Not many kids lived on the huge estate. We all knew each other, at least by sight. The memory of his persuasive presence in my mind had me unnerved in ways I couldn't explain. My body betrayed the anxiety with sweaty palms and a racing heart.

Missy avoided my eyes, something a lot of people did unintentionally, thinking it would keep me from reading their minds.

'She shouldn't have seen that... hope she doesn't say anything... I could get in trouble... don't want her to get in trouble either... sweet girl.'

"Oh, don't worry about him, love. Now you'd better be going. Headmaster Higgins doesn't like to be kept waiting."

"Of course. Have a good day, Missy."

Her face relaxed. "You too, Sam."

I opened the door to leave the clinic, but stopped when I noticed Dr. Sato in the hall talking with a new doctor I didn't recognize. Her face squinted in anger and her arms flailed about as she made her point. He looked even angrier and spoke to her in a low, mean voice, and took a step forward, his hand held up in a way that made me flinch in fear for her.

I slipped into his mind and—something shoved me out and slammed the door! My head pounded like it had been pummeled with an anvil. That had never happened before. The doctor looked at me and his rage melted into a smile, a gleam of gold tooth shining from his mouth. My insides turned to Jell-O as his aura seduced me into complacency, but then the urgent plea for help from Mystery Boy pushed out the unwelcome intrusion. The doctor had some kind of para-power, and he was immune to mine.

Shock flooded my system. And fear. No one had ever been immune to my mind-reading. A trail of dread crawled up my spine and wound itself around my heart.

I fled to the comfort of the outdoors.

The sun felt ten shades brighter than normal outside the double glass doors. I pulled my sunglasses out of my backpack and walked the winding trails through campus, my body still shaking from both unusual encounters. The warmth calmed me, but not enough to erase the effects of that strange boy and his compelling mind, not to mention the creepy doctor.

***

Near the main offices, a group of kids ran by in gym uniforms. One petite girl fell out of line to throw herself into a hug.

"Lucy!" I laughed and hugged her back just as fiercely.

"Where have you been, Chica? And what the hell happened to your face?"

Even in gym clothes, my best friend could cause a riot with her curvy figure, smooth brown skin, and long, dark Spanish hair.

"Lucy, let's go!" Luke waved at me as he called his sister. They fell behind their class. "Hey, Sam, meet us tonight, okay? We need to talk." His face pinched in a frown.

"Sure thing." I pushed Lucy away. "Go, I'll see you later. I have to get to the office."

"Fine, but I want details. And we really do need to talk."

She ran off, her ponytail swinging down her back. Though tempted to spy on her mind to find out what had both of them so upset, I needed to get to Higgins's office. Besides, I'd see them later, and could fill them in on my adventures. The rules didn't allow us to share the details of our assignments with anyone, not even other paranormals. But Luke, Lucy and I had been best friends since we could remember, and we found ways to communicate without technically breaking those rules—like a secret language I'd created several years ago.

I walked on, my mind drifting. Oh, Tommy. How I wished I could have told him the truth, told him everything about my life.

What would Tommy have said if he'd known who I really was? It made me sad to think about.

I shook off my melancholy and entered the headmaster's office.

He didn't stand, or even look up at me, when his secretary ushered me into his office, just stared down at his oh-so-important papers.

She closed the door, and I settled into one of the chairs in front of his desk and reluctantly took off my sunglasses. My face would further condemn my actions. After a moment, he looked up.

"Ah, Sam, you look wretched. How are you feeling?"

Not the opening I had expected. "Bit of a headache. I'll be okay."

He already had the oral briefing, but I followed standard procedure. I'd been given time before the drugs to complete my written report on the plane, and I placed that on his desk

He flipped through it, then shuffled the papers that had consumed his attention a moment ago and placed them neatly in his filing drawer.

I fidgeted with the zipper on my book bag. I wanted to ask about the art contest, and the interview, but I didn't dare jump the gun after involving the Feds in my assignment and threatening a client.

"You know that stunt you pulled could have gotten this entire organization in trouble," he said.

"I know. And I wish I could say I'm sorry, but you don't know what he was thinking, what Beaumont was going to do to that girl—and other girls. Honestly, this is the biggest creep I've ever met. I had to make sure he didn't get away."

"You've always been one of our best, never causing problems. This is your first mistake, so I'm going to let it slide. But this is a once-in-a-lifetime freebie. Any more trouble and I won't be so nice."

"I know." My whole body relaxed, releasing the tension I hadn't been aware I carried.

"Good. Well, I have some exciting news for you."

Oh?

"You've been accepted into Sarah Lawrence College." He pulled out an official-looking letter and handed it to me.

"Oh my God, really? But how? I haven't even had the interview yet?"

"I called in a favor. I wasn't sure if you'd be back in time and I didn't want you to miss out on this chance at your dreams. Based on the portfolio you sent in, a nudge from me and a glowing evaluation from Mr. Krevner, they agreed to let you in without the required interview."

I stared down at the fancy parchment paper, unable to fully digest the news. *Dear Sam Smith, It is our pleasure to inform you that you have been accepted to the undergraduate visual art program at Sarah Lawrence College....*

"Smith? That was the best you could do?" I laughed, clutching the letter that represented my entire future.

"It's a good name. It's common and doesn't draw attention to you, all the things you want when you finally enter that life."

"It's fine, I'll take it. Thank you, Headmaster Higgins."

"You're welcome, Sam. You deserve it. You've been one of our best and brightest students. We'll be sad to see you go. That reminds me," he pulled out another file, "this job just came in, and I think you'd be perfect for it."

He handed me the brief. I flipped through it: two kids with para-powers had been beaten and nearly killed at a prep school in New York. I needed to infiltrate the school and see if any other paranormals attended. I also needed to track down the perpetrators. Not so bad. At least I'd be in New York and helping kids like me—but, wait. *Oh God. I so do not want this job.*

"Mary? You're sending me off with Mary? You've got to be kidding me. She's horrible. And what's she supposed to do, seduce the teachers? I can handle this alone, or send Lucy with me. She's great at these kinds of assignments. Anyone but Mary."

"I'm sorry, Sam, but Mary has some unique skills that could come in handy, especially as it's likely that one of the leaders is a man. You'll need her with you."

"But I just got back! And you promised that was my last assignment before I left. I have to pack and complete my studies. I want to spend time with my friends, and there's the art contest!"

"You have a few months before you need to leave. It shouldn't take you long, and it will give you some extra cash for your new life. I'm throwing in a $10,000 bonus if you complete this assignment without any problems."

"That doesn't help with my art contest. I don't have time to do this and prepare."

Higgins looked down at his desk, shoulders slumped.

Uh-oh.

'How to tell her.... Will break her heart.... Wish I could skip this.'

"Tell me what?"

He looked me in the eyes, the way a doctor looks at someone whose loved one has died.

"I have some bad news. There was an accident in the art building while you were gone. There's a lot of flammable material there and — we don't know what happened yet, but somehow... a fire started. Sam — "

"No! Stop. This is insane. I don't want to hear this."

"Sam, your painting. I'm so sorry."

I grabbed my book bag and ran out his door and toward the art studio. I heard the headmaster follow me but didn't turn to acknowledge him. I had to see the damage for myself.

On the outside, the building looked fine. A small sigh of relief escaped my lips. Surely it couldn't be that bad. Maybe I'd have to repair some smoke damage or something, but I could handle that. Mr. K would help me.

I moved aside a yellow ribbon that marked the building as unsafe and walked into the dimly lit studio.

And stopped breathing.

The inside of the building had been gutted and turned to ash. I choked on a strangled cry.

Higgins put his hand on my shoulder. "I'm sorry, Sam. Nothing survived."

The remains of my painting stood in the corner. I examined the charred bits that had been my greatest work and couldn't stop the tears from flowing.

Higgins tried again to comfort me, but I pushed him away. "Where's Mr. K?"

"Sam, let's just go back to my office and talk about this."

Panic stirred in my heart. I raised my voice in desperation. "Where's Mr. K?"

"He quit. After the fire, he couldn't stand to be here anymore, and he left. He's gone, Sam, and won't be coming back."

"No, that can't be true. He'd never leave me, not without saying goodbye. Not before I graduated. You're lying. What did you do? Where is he?" I ran through the studio, searching for my mentor, but no sign remained of him. All traces of his work, his passion, his presence—gone.

I sank to my knees and sobbed. Everything I'd ever created, all of my artistic expression, had been housed in this studio. My entire portfolio was gone, just like Mr. K. Destroyed. I only had some pictures of the best pieces, but almost none of the originals. My entire life's work to date.

"I need to be alone."

Higgins left me without a word and I cried into the ash.

CHAPTER 10 – SAM

Luke walked through my door to wake me up. He'd have been toast if my para-power included super strength or kickass reactions. Instead, he got to suffer through my weeping. He probably would have preferred the fight.

He unlocked my door from the inside and let Lucy in, then closed and locked the door again.

My suite wasn't as grand as theirs, but it had everything I needed as a fully stocked and decorated studio apartment, complete with mini kitchen.

I didn't budge from my bed, nor did I acknowledge my best friends, but that didn't deter them.

Luke pulled the covers off me and crawled into bed next to me. Lucy joined him on the other side and spoke softly, as if to a frightened kitten. "He told you?"

I nodded, unable to speak just yet.

"Did you see the damage?"

Another nod.

"Luke snuck in. He tried to salvage some of it, but...."

My voice came out in a crackle. "I know. I saw."

"And Mr. K. We have no idea what happened to him. We never saw him after the fire. I confronted Higgins about it. He says Mr. K quit, but Sam... he's lying."

That got my attention. If Mr. K didn't quit, did Higgins fire him and lie to me?

"Doesn't matter. I'm not doing art anymore."

"Don't say that! You're a brilliant artist and you can't give up just because something bad happened. You have all that art in you, everything you've ever created or will create. Don't let this steal your gift."

A melancholy seeped into my soul and quenched whatever small flame Lucy's pep talk might have ignited. Nothing mattered anymore.

Luke, in an attempt to change the subject, gently brushed my swollen face. "What happened?"

"I mouthed off to a client, and he punched me."

Their eyebrows shot up in comical unison. Luke glanced at Lucy, and she nodded her head. "She's telling the truth, more or less. But she's definitely not telling us the whole story."

"Hey, quit reading me!" I lightly punched Lucy on the shoulder, grateful to be talking about something other than my ruined art career. I pulled my red comforter over my head, as if that would keep her out of my secrets. No such luck.

"Sam, what's going on?" Lucy's voice lost its playfulness. "You've never talked back to a client before. Not even that guy who kept undressing you with his mind, and then dressing you back up in his wife's lingerie."

I'd forgotten about him. He was a real winner too. No one should ever have to see themselves naked in the mind of a pervert. I shivered at the memory and mentally closed my third eye to shut out the experience.

"Tell us." Luke spoke our secret language, the one I had created. It had evolved over the years to include thousands of words. So I told them everything—about the assignment, the molester, Tommy, Mary at the hospital.

"She's such a bitch," Luke said.

Gotta love Luke, though Mary sure didn't. She hated the one heterosexual man in all the world that her powers didn't affect. No one knew why, but we were grateful.

Lucy eyed me, no doubt waiting for the rest of the story. I scowled at her, but finally relented. I told them about the boy on the stretcher and the strange doctor with para-powers.

"Sam, you cannot get involved in whatever that is. You know that, right?" Lucy adopted the rigid face of Mrs. Kellerbuckle, the eighth-grade taskmaster at Rent-A-Kid. It was usually funny when she did that. This time, not so much.

"Yeah, I'm not. It was just weird, is all."

She shook her head. "Not totally the truth, though I think you believe your own lie at the moment. Just promise me you'll talk to us before doing anything stupid?"

"I promise."

Before they could start on me again, I slid over Luke and put in our favorite movie, "X-Men," and we settled in for some mindless entertainment. I pretended to ignore the voice in the back of my head that spoke of things best left forgotten.

***

All eyes were on me the next day at school, with the rumor mill full of juicy tidbits about my black eye, the fire in the art building, and the sudden disappearance of Mr. K. I kept my sunglasses on and hid behind Luke as often as possible.

When I bumped into him for the fifth time, he turned to face me. "Sam, I love you, and I know you're embarrassed, but if you bump me again, I'm going to have to walk through a wall to make it to class on time. Got it?"

I nodded and mumbled an apology. He softened and put an arm around me.

Lucy flanked me on the other side. "It doesn't look that bad. Honest."

"I don't need to be able to read minds or tell when someone is lying to know that's a big fat one."

She squeezed my shoulder. "Well, Chica, it could be worse. And it will get better. You should just ignore it and go on like everything is normal. People are only staring because you're acting so weird about it."

She's probably right. But with a mild case of OCD, I couldn't resist popping into people's minds as we walked down the halls to English.

'Wonder what happened to her?'... 'Heard she got punched by a client.'... 'Looks painful.'... 'She must have really screwed up.'... 'I wonder if Higgins punished her.'... 'I heard she got into a fight with a new kid... and he's been in the infirmary ever since.'

That last thought stopped me. Were they thinking of my mystery boy? I searched the crowd of teenagers to see who'd thought that, probing minds as I did. Everyone rushed to get books out of lockers and head to their next class before the bell rang. I couldn't pinpoint the person, but it gave me hope.

Lucy pulled me along. "What's the matter? We're going to be late."

"Sorry, just caught a stray thought that bothered me."

"Don't worry about what people are saying, or thinking. You'll be old news in no time flat. Besides, you won't even be here much longer, and none of this will matter."

No more thoughts came up about the boy, but the school was abuzz about the fire. Anyone with a penchant or para-power for fire became a suspect. When Lucy and Luke left me, I just ignored everyone, hid in the bathroom, and applied another layer of cover-up to my bruise, but hiding was no use.

Mary and her pack entered the bathroom chattering away.

I scurried into a stall to avoid her, but not in time.

Her hand wrapped around my arm and pulled me out before I could close the door. "If it isn't the little kiss-ass hiding in the bathroom. What? Afraid you might scare the younger kids with your new look?"

I backed away from Mary, fear of conflict once again ruling me. But something snapped. The small fire that had started when I stood up to Dollinger now flamed to life. I stepped forward, for the first time invading Mary's personal space, and stared her in the eyes, so close her breath crawled over my skin. Power flooded me and I finally felt in control. This dwarfed even the rush I'd felt by the pool.

"What is your problem, Mary? Honestly, what do you gain by tormenting me? Does it stroke your fragile self-esteem? Are you so pathetic that only hurting other people makes you feel better? Do you really think that makes you hot shit?"

I didn't wait for her to reply. "Well, you know what, I don't really care anymore. Say what you want, it makes no difference."

Her eyes narrowed and her mouthed dropped open. Not the response she'd expected.

Her two lackeys held onto frozen sneers, waiting to see what would happen.

"And here's a tip for you. Don't mess with a girl who reads minds. I can pull out every thought you've ever had. What do you think I'll find if I do that? I can tell you what everyone else thinks of you too. Do you think the guys at this school really like you? That your powers make real feelings? You're fooling yourself, Mary, but no one else. They despise you for what you do to them." My voice sounded ugly, nothing like the real me—at least, the me I'd always imagined. Yet the raw righteousness of it, of feeding her the bile she always spewed at us, was like peeling off an itchy scab.

Her face collapsed, and she ran out of the bathroom, followed by her friends.

I sank onto the nearest toilet, shaking. Out of fear, rage, guilt? Standing up to her didn't feel as good as expected.

Maybe I felt bad because it felt so good, if that made any sense at all.

But something inside me rose up to greet this new girl who wouldn't allow herself to be pushed around, and against my own better judgment, I thought of my mystery boy.

***

I lost track of how long I sat in the bathroom, alone in my thoughts. When a group of giggling girls came in, I slid past them and out into the crowded halls of my school.

The bustle of life and my swirling thoughts made it hard to focus on anything. The adrenaline surge from my confrontation with Mary had long since passed, leaving me shaky and tired. My head ached and my eye pounded a steady pulse of pain with each heartbeat.

A familiar tug pulled at me, beckoning me to hide out in my room and cocoon myself from the harsh realities of life, but I couldn't. I first had to figure out what had happened to the art studio and my mentor.

With this renewed determination as armor against my pain, I focused my mind to search for the one person who might have some answers.

Kyle. The only fire starter in school.

His mental signature led me out of the building and through the gardens and walking paths near The Hub. I found him slumped over on a bench, lighting his finger like a lighter and then blowing it out. Light, blow, repeat.

"Kyle, can I talk to you?"

Though I'd kept my voice calm, he still jumped out of his seat and let loose a small ball of flames into the air. His eyes widened in fear at the loss of control, and he quickly diffused it before it could start any bigger fires.

"Sam, I heard you were back. I'm sorry about what happened... with your art."

I gestured to the bench. "May I join you?"

His eyes shuffled back and forth like a man hunted, but he nodded.

I settled in next to him and tried to maintain eye contact despite his shifting gaze. "You know I can read your mind whether you're looking at me or not."

"Sorry. It's just... I know everyone thinks I caused the fire, but I swear, I didn't."

'Don't know anything... but sensed something that night.... No one believes me.... Think I don't have control.'

"I believe you, Kyle. Can you tell me what you sensed that night?"

His golden eyes dropped, leaving me to stare at his auburn scalp.

"Okay, look. I know this sounds weird, but I can sense if there's a fire around. It's like, my body tingles or something." He looked back up, perhaps to judge my reaction.

I kept a neutral face and encouraged him to continue.

With more confidence, he did. "I can also tell something about the fire. Like, I know in my bones if it's manmade or natural or what, you know?"

"Makes sense."

"So, okay, that night, something weird happened. Like, that fire didn't just happen by accident. Someone started it on purpose."

"It was arson?" I had no room left in me for fear or shock, only a numb sadness.

"Yeah, but more than that. See, the fire started with power. Like, someone else who has a power like mine started it."

This shoved away some of the numb. "Another fire starter?"

"Yes and no. Like me but not. Fire starting's not their real, full power. It's like they were stealing the power from somewhere else. Then I felt it."

"What?"

"The draining. They stole the power from me. So you see? It really was my fault. I'm so sorry, Sam."

Tears filled his eyes and he dropped his head again to hide his pain, but it still washed over me in thoughts and feelings and images. I opened myself and let everything he thought and felt hit me. Then I took all that raw data and shoved it into a special compartment in my own mind to examine later.

I reached for Kyle's hand. "It's not your fault. Whoever did this stole your power... you can't be held responsible for that. Thank you for telling me."

He looked up with something akin to hope in his eyes. We all needed forgiveness for our sins, perceived or real. We all craved absolution, so I gave him his.

"It's okay, Kyle. I'll figure out what happened. It's not your fault. But, don't tell anyone else this, all right? At least not until I uncover the truth about that night."

A buzzing filled me, and I left him to his thoughts as I walked through the winding paths without purpose or destination. Someone had stolen another para-power and burned up my work.

Why would anyone do that? And who could possibly have that kind of power?

I needed to find out, and I needed help.

CHAPTER 11 – DRAKE

Awareness flickered in and out like pinpricks of light through a torn window curtain. Voices, footsteps, the clank of metal, the medicinal smell that permeated his dreams—these small, mundane sounds woke Drake from his unconscious visions and pulled him from the blue-eyed girl in his mind.

The thump of his heart seemed abnormally loud, and for a moment he wondered if he had died and gone to some limbo place where grey souls lived. But no, not dead—the sound belonged to a monitor attached to him, broadcasting the rhythmic beat of his heart to the world.

He focused on keeping the sound steady as he opened his eyes to take in his surroundings. The unremarkable hospital room gave him no sense of place or time.

A tickle itched his nose and he moved his arm to scratch it, only to find that he couldn't move. His limbs had been restrained to the hospital bed: two thick straps across his legs, a strap across his chest and a strap to tie down each wrist.

An I.V. dripped a viscous yellow solution into his veins and created a mild burn that ran up his arm and through his body. The door to his room was closed, so he focused his powers to surge through his muscles and free him from his prison.

Pain flashed through him like fire in his blood, and his strength abandoned him.

He lay on the bed panting, wrung out and useless. He fought, pulled, flexed, and lifted himself in an effort to overcome the effects of the drug, to no avail. His efforts won him not freedom, but rather several burns and cuts into his skin. They would heal soon enough, if the drug didn't inhibit that part of him as well.

Defeated, he relaxed into the bed and wondered how he'd let himself get caught. He should have listened to Father Patrick and Brad. He should've known he'd never be allowed to live his dreams.

These thoughts fanned the fires of his rage, but that fire had no will, no power to grow. Exhausted, Drake slept... and dreamt.

***

He sits on the bed, as still as a mouse — as still as a dead mouse, his new daddy would say. Dead mice can't move. Dead boys can't move either, so Drake doesn't move a single muscle. He doesn't want to be a dead boy.

New Daddy will be home soon. New Mommy locks herself in her room with the bottles that smell funny. She won't come out again, Drake knows. She won't help him, not like his real mommy who smelled like roses and laughed a lot, except that last night.

Real Mommy and Daddy gave lots of hugs and cuddles and let him eat ice cream on special days. They loved Drake, but they weren't strong like him, and when the car made the awful crunching sounds, and their blood got all over him, he watched as the light in their eyes faded to nothing.

They died and left him.

Now he will die if he isn't very careful. So Drake sits still and he waits.

When the front door crashes open, he inhales sharply, but doesn't make a peep. Not one. If he lies down or tries to hide, New Daddy will be even madder.

New Daddy starts shouting in the living room and throwing things against the wall. Soon, New Daddy will come to Drake's room. Soon, it will be Drake's turn.

Still, he waits.

His bedroom door flies open and New Daddy stands there, big and mean and scary and smelling like those bottles and cigarettes. "You've been a bad boy, son. It's time to take your punishment."

Drake squeezes his eyes shut and stays very quiet.

When the blows come, he doesn't make a sound.

When the fist lands on his face and the pain explodes in his head, he still doesn't move.

When it's over, he's allowed to lie down, finally.

New Daddy leaves and closes the door.

Drake cries silently into his pillow.

New Daddy knows Drake is strong, stronger than other four-year-olds. New Daddy knows Drake will heal.

And Drake knows New Daddy will be back.

Someday, Drake will be ready for New Daddy.

***

The wild beating of Drake's heart woke him with a jolt, sweat beading his forehead. He couldn't control the *thrump-thrump-thrump* as his heartbeat accelerated in panic.

A nurse rushed in, needle in hand as if brandishing a weapon. Her eyes widened in surprise and fear. "You're awake. You shouldn't be."

He ignored the stupidity of her comment. "Where am I? Why have you kidnapped and imprisoned me?"

She frowned in confusion. "We didn't kidnap you, we saved you."

He sneers at her. "From what? A surfing victory? Thanks so much for that."

She shuffled away from him, though she hadn't come close enough for him to reach her. "The doctor will be here any minute. He'll explain everything. But you're lucky we found you in time. You could have died."

She looked at the needle in her hand, then capped and pocketed it and left as quickly as she had come.

Guess she didn't want to get too close.

Drake counted the tiles on the browning ceiling as he waited for the doctor, though he doubted he'd get an honest answer from anyone here.

A moment later, a tall man with bushy eyebrows walked in. "I'm Dr. Pana, your treating physician. The nurse tells me you think we kidnapped you."

The doctor's smooth-as-glass voice wrapped itself around Drake like velvet. His will weakened, for just a moment, and the good doctor almost cracked Drake's defenses and wormed his way in. Almost.

"I was drugged, knocked out, and strapped down against my will. What would *you* call it?"

A caterpillar eyebrow shot up in surprise, the only evidence that the doctor had underestimated Drake's ability to resist him. "A new organization is bent on destroying anyone with unique gifts such as yours. They targeted you and would have killed you had we not intervened in time. We're keeping you here for your own safety, and, given the nature of your gifts and some of your past deeds, we found it necessary to restrain you for the staff's safety. We have to make sure you are stable and safe, Mr. Davis, before we can release you."

"Where am I?"

"You're being cared for in an undisclosed private facility where anyone intending you harm cannot track you. Now I suggest you take advantage of this time to rest and heal."

Dr. Pana pressed the nurse's buzzer. "Please bring the patient's medicine."

When the nurse returned, she shook as if scared, but Drake didn't think he was the cause. She cast furtive glances at Dr. Pana as she reached over with a needle and inserted the syringe into his I.V. "Rest now."

Euphoria flooded Drake's system and erased all thoughts of escape and all feelings of fear.

Dr. Pana smiled, and a gold tooth glinted in the fluorescent lights. "See you soon, Mr. Davis."

CHAPTER 12 – SAM

Sleep came slowly that night, and when I finally surrendered to my dreams they were filled with horrible beatings, car crashes, blood, and a little boy who fought his way to be free of abuse.

My heart broke for the blond boy in my dreams. He reminded me of Tommy, and I wanted to comfort him, to rescue him and give him hope.

Perhaps he represented my inner child, the inner artist in me who needed to be free to create and express? Except, it didn't feel like that at all, it felt more like a memory that would haunt me forever.

Lucy and Luke met me for breakfast in our cafeteria that morning, and I told them about my dream.

Luke shoved a spoonful of cheerios into his mouth before speaking. "You're just stressed. You need to unwind. Come spar with me and Lucy. We'll work out that extra tension."

"More like beat it out of me. No thanks." I looked around to make sure no one could hear me before bringing up what I really wanted to talk to them about.

"Listen, I need your help. Someone on campus is stealing other people's powers and using them." This got their attention and they both leaned in to listen.

I told them about my conversation with Kyle.

Lucy pursed her lips. "He could have been lying."

I scoffed. "I might not be a human lie detector, but I dug pretty deep into his mind. He wasn't lying."

Luke tapped his long fingers on the table. "This is bad. No one's come forward with this kind of power. I have a hard time believing it's a student. Could one of the staff have a power we never realized before?"

I thought back to my brief encounter with the mysterious doctor with the gold tooth. "That doctor had some kind of power. Maybe it's him. He arrives out of the blue, and all of the sudden a boy shows up beaten, and someone steals Kyle's fire power to burn down the studio—not to mention Mr. K leaves without even saying goodbye. Don't you find that a bit too coincidental? And Higgins is lying to us, too."

Before they could reply, Mary and her gang walked past and shoved me into my tray of food, splashing milk and juice into my lap.

She giggled, and her lackeys followed suit. "Oops, sorry about that. Didn't see you there."

Lucy sprang from her seat. "Oh no you don't, bitch." She grabbed Mary's long blond hair and pulled it back. "You're going to apologize to Sam, now."

Enough was enough. I faced Mary but spoke to Lucy. "Let her go. I can handle this."

Lucy narrowed her eyes like a cat ready to attack, but did as I asked.

My voice came out low, but firm. "You don't learn, do you? I wasn't kidding, Mary. I'm done with your crap."

I looked to the girl on her right. "Roberta, did you know that Mary deliberately seduced your boyfriend last year so that he'd break up with you? She was jealous and couldn't stand for you to be happy."

Roberta's grin collapsed in on itself, and she stepped back from Mary.

"And Caroline, remember those awful rumors about you earlier this year? How horrible you felt for months? Mary started them because you were getting more popular than her."

Both girls eyed their leader with venomous looks.

Mary shot daggers into me, but she knew her powers were nothing compared to mine. "You're going to pay for this, Sam."

"What are you going to do? Seduce me? Give it up, Mary. I can do a lot worse than this, and I will if you don't stop bullying people."

Inside I started shaking again. This behavior felt so hateful, but also necessary. She'd tortured the student body enough.

It took a moment for me to realize that other students had stood and started clapping. The guys looked relieved—likely they'd suffered the worse, having their natural instincts and hormones turned against them every time she was near.

Once again I was so grateful Luke had immunity to her powers of seduction. I couldn't bear the thought of him being under her thrall.

Mary pushed through the crowd and stormed off alone.

The clapping subsided and I collapsed into myself. "Let's get out of here."

Luke and Lucy had phys ed training, but I had the rest of the day free.

Before we parted ways, Lucy hugged me. "I'm so proud of you, Chica! You finally stood up for yourself in a totally badass way!"

But I wasn't listening to Lucy. My attention had been claimed by another voice, one inside my head.

A soft whisper stole my breath. *'You did good. I'm proud of you, too.'*

My mystery boy was awake, and he could talk to me.

***

"*Can you hear me?*" My heart skipped beats as I waited.

'Yes.'

I nearly fell to the ground. In all my years as a mind reader, I'd never had a two-way conversation with anyone. A lot of firsts in the mind-reading business lately.

"*Who are you? Can you read minds too?*"

'My name is Drake, and no, I can't. Are you the girl with the blue eyes?'

Drake. I rolled his name around in my mind. A strong, sexy name; I liked it. Did he remember me from our brief contact before he passed out? "*I'm a girl with blue eyes, but not the only one.*"

He mentally chuckled, and the sound warmed me from the inside. *'I saw you, before they took me into the hospital room. How are we able to do this?'*

"*I honestly don't know. Do you have powers?*" He must, to be here at all.

He hesitated. I knew that with the smallest push I could find out for myself, but I wanted him to trust me, to open up to me.

"*I can control minds, and I'm strong. Someone kidnapped me and brought me here. I need to get out. Where are we?*"

A girl behind me nudged me. "Are you going in?"

We stood in front of my dorm, but I didn't remember walking there. "Sorry, lost in thought." I walked into the main hall and up to my room.

Once there, I locked the door behind me and closed the curtains. This felt too private for any kind of exposure.

"What do you mean someone kidnapped you?"

He told me about the day of his surfing competition and how he was attacked.

"Did they tell you why?"

'Something about saving me from another group who tried to hurt me.'

That made sense, and jived with what Higgins had said, though the headmaster was no longer the beacon of honesty I had once thought.

I told him what I knew about the group attacking paranormals, and described Rent-A-Kid and my life as best I could.

'So you think they really are trying to help me? I gotta say, while you seem on the up and up, the doctor who treated me does not. I can smell a rat a mile away, and he's a very bad dude.'

He couldn't be talking about Dr. Sato, but I could guess whom he meant.

"Did this doctor happen to have a gold tooth and oily personality?"

'The very one. Know him?'

"Not intimately. I saw him in the hall yelling at our regular doctor the day I met you. Drake, I couldn't read him, not at all. That's never happened before."

And so I told him everything. About Mr. K and my painting and my assignment with Tommy.

For a moment, the absurdity of my situation hit me. I was talking to a voice in my head. If not for all that I'd already seen, I'd be worried about my sanity.

If Drake had been standing in front of me, there's no way I'd have been this transparent and vulnerable. But our unique way of communicating made it so much easier to trust him — after all, he was just a voice in my mind. Talking to him was like thinking — just as natural.

As the day wore into night, we kept up a steady stream of dialogue, discussing everything from our favorite food and favorite color to our deepest fears and most secret hopes. Through his memories, I saw the many foster homes he'd grown up in and the church with towering angels in a magical garden.

I showed him different assignments I'd been on and the countries I'd traveled to. We talked about Hawaii and surfing and art and college.

Even in moments of silence, his thoughts swirled into mine like vanilla and chocolate ice cream melting into each other.

With him, I felt the same comfort and familiarity as I did with Luke. They both had a protective quality that made me feel safe, but Drake did not inspire any brotherly feelings at all. Quite the opposite.

I'd always assumed that for chemistry between two people to ignite, they had to be physically present with one another. After all, didn't their pheromones have to sniff each other out or something?

But with Drake, even just mentally, science and magic combined to create something new and wonderful. The warmth of those new feelings spread through my body as his deep voice seduced my mind and heart.

Within twenty-four hours of near non-stop communication, Drake and I had created a bond that I'd never found with anyone else, even after years of friendship. This is the power of the mind, the power of thoughts — and the power of emotions.

***

Drake stayed with me throughout my classes the next day. He helped keep me awake after being up for two days, and nearly got me in trouble a few times with his smart-ass remarks about my teachers, fellow students or classes.

By the time I arrived at Luke and Lucy's suite after school, I was dead on my feet.

Lucy eyed me up and down and brewed some coffee. I curled up on their overstuffed chair and listened as Drake told me a story about Father Patrick, a man I couldn't wait to meet, based on what I knew so far.

Luke threw a pillow at me. "Yo, Sam, where are you?"

I realized I'd ignored them again. It was time to introduce them to Drake. "I'm sorry. Um, remember that mystery boy I told you about? I'm talking to him right now."

Lucy nearly dropped the coffee pot. "Shut up! Seriously? When did this happen. You can't just let random guys into your mind, Sam."

Right, like this happened every day. There goes Sam, the mind whore.

I explained about how we connected and our night and day together.

Lucy sat on the couch across from me and handed me a mug of coffee. "No wonder you look like something a dog spit out."

"Gee, thanks, you're sweet."

Luke poured a cup for himself and sat next to Lucy. "So he's here, right now? Can he hear us?"

"Yes, he can hear what I can. He's basically hearing my thoughts, not so much you. But don't worry guys, I've spent hours and hours talking with him, exploring his mind. I know we can trust him."

Lucy frowned in disapproval. "He could be playing you, Sam, trying to get into your mind to hurt you. With everything that's happened recently, do you really think it's a good idea to let a stranger in like this?"

"If you can't trust him, then you have to trust me. I know him—yes, even after only one night, I know him. He can help us, and with everything that's going on, we need the help."

Lucy's eyes widened. "You're in love with him. Oh my God, Sam, you're in love!"

Heat flooded my face. "Stop! We are close, and I'll admit to some... feeling." Oh my God, this was such an embarrassing conversation to have with him listening.

He chuckled in my mind, and I wanted to mentally swat him, but that just made him chuckle harder.

"Let's just see how it goes, but for now, you don't need to worry. He's not a spy and he's not trying to hurt me. He wants to help."

I stared them both down, and while they didn't fall into immediate trust with Drake, they were willing to try.

I did a mental victory dance. "Okay, let's focus. Something's going on here, and we need to figure out what it is. It's time to create our own assignment. You in?"

Lucy stood and stretched. "You know I am. We obviously can't sit by and do nothing."

We both looked to Luke.

He grinned like the Cheshire Cat. "Seriously, do you even have to ask?"

I smiled. "Okay, here's the plan. I'm going to go back to the studio and dig through the rubble in Mr. K's office to see if I can find any clues. I just have this sense that in our last class together he was trying to tell me something, and I need to figure out what. Luke, see if you can dig up any dirt in Higgins's office, and Lucy, you're the interrogator. Question students, faculty, even Higgins if you can. Also, scope out the clinic and figure out who's lying. We'll meet back here tonight to compare notes."

'*How can I help?*'

How could Drake help? He was strapped down and powerless, though I didn't say that to him. I could only imagine how impotent he felt right now. "*Find out what you can from the nurses and Dr. Pana if you see him again. He's the key here.*"

"Be careful, everyone, and remember that Rent-A-Kid is watching us. Don't raise too much suspicion."

***

The wind whipped my ponytail across my face and chilled me to the bone, but still I didn't move to open the door to the studio. I couldn't. My plan had sounded good in the comfort of Luke and Lucy's suite, but now, standing alone to face the remains of my life's work... my enthusiasm for this mission waned.

'*Are you okay?*'

"*No, not really. Whoever burned down this studio turned my dreams to ash as well. I mean, I still have school, but without my art....*"

A flash of emotion seared me, and a memory stormed my senses. The taste of the sea, the feel of the sun and wind, the surf under my board... wait, not my board, Drake's. I'd never been surfing, but in that moment I knew exactly how it felt to ride a wave and let go of all the pain and fear, all the social expectations and the need to hide my true self in public.

In one blow, that dream died as they dragged me—him—away.

A tear slid down my cheek. I wasn't the only one mourning the loss of a dream. "*I'm sorry.*"

'*You're not alone, I just wanted you to know that. And someday, when I have my powers back and am free,*

I'm going to do some serious damage to the people who've hurt you.'

His words released in me a primal urge to feel safe and protected, to belong to someone in a more intimate way than I'd ever experienced before. Still, in that moment he was just a voice, and I had to do this on my own.

I opened the door and stepped in. Raw pain filled me at the sight of my painting.

'Show me what it looked like, before the fire.'

His request surprised me, but I did as he asked. With eyes closed, I projected the exact details of the painting I had poured my soul into. Just as I had experienced his love of surfing in a visceral way, he shared not just the visual beauty of my work, but the love and passion with which I had dedicated myself to it.

'Thank you. Now, it will never truly be gone.'

I choked back a sob and went to Mr. K's office. I pulled my sketchbook out of my book bag and ran my hand over the cover with the gold emblem, then opened it to the sketch I'd drawn from his mind the last time I'd seen him.

The box had been important. It had to be here somewhere.

I searched his desk, his cubby and his metal filing cabinet, but found nothing of note. His office had survived the fire with less damage than the studio, but it didn't reveal any secrets that would help. Frustrated, I fell into his chair and put my head on his metal desk. That's when I noticed the painting on the wall. It had been moved and hung slightly askew.

No way. That was too clichéd even for Mr. K. But... what if?

I went over and moved aside the painting. Sure enough, he had a safe.

Now what? What combination of numbers would be most important to Mr. K? I thought back to all the times I'd read his mind for assignments. Piece by piece, I recalled numbers that stood out. 4-15-70, the date he'd lost his wife and child in a freak accident.

The safe clicked open and inside sat my box.

I ran my hands over the delicate detail of the carving; he'd done the work himself. Grief threatened to overcome me. I missed him so much. No one had ever understood me or my passions the way he had.

The box didn't open on first try. It had been locked, but I couldn't find a spot for the key. The box didn't have a keyhole, but an emblem—fit to complement the one on my journal—adorned its front.

Using a metal letter opener from the desk, I pried the emblem off my sketchbook and inserted it into the emblem on the box. With a firm twist, it opened. I held my breath in anticipation of what I would find.

Nothing. The box was empty.

I turned it upside down, as if gravity would magically spill the secrets I'd hoped it would contain, but of course, nothing fell out.

Crushed, I couldn't contain the tears anymore. Sobs tore through me and I unleashed all my rage and fear and grief. I nearly threw the box across the room, but stopped myself in time. Mr. K had made this; it was all I had left of him.

"What am I going to do, Drake? I can't live with the loss of both Mr. K and my art."

'We'll find a way, Sam. I promise. Have you checked for any secret compartments in the box? When I lived in foster care I had to hide things important to me, and that's how I did it.'

Excitement overcame me and I looked on the box with new eyes. The inside didn't seem as deep as it should have been. Using the same letter opener, I loosened the bottom on all sides until it popped off.

A letter lay in the compartment, and it had my name written on it in a familiar scrawl.

~~~

Sam,

If you're reading this, I'm gone. Please know I would never leave you here alone, which means I didn't leave voluntarily. There are deep secrets at this school, and I've only scratched the surface. One of my students disappeared after she left. She's not where Higgins said she'd be. I fear a worse fate for you. Get out, Sam. However you can, get out. Someday, if I'm still alive, I'll find you.

You were the best of them all.

Mr. K

P.S. I made this box for you. Keep your own secrets in it.

~~~

What had Mr. K discovered that scared him so much, and what did they do to him?

"*Drake, did you see?*"

'*Yes. Do you believe me now? They kidnapped me, Sam. They didn't save me from shit!*'

"*I don't know. Yes. Maybe. It's all so much. I wish I knew what to do. I wish Mr. K was still here.*"

Luke and Lucy needed to see this. I put the letter back and sealed it, then slipped the box into my bag.

I left Mr. K's office and walked right into Headmaster Higgins.

"Sam, what are you doing here?"

"I came to see if any of my art survived. The first time, I was too upset."

His face softened. "Of course. Actually, I'm glad I ran into you. The clinic is looking for you. It's time for your vitamin shot and checkup."

"Right now?" I had a standing appointment every three months for that, and this was odd timing.

"Yes, they've revamped the vitamin cocktail, and we need to make sure all the students get it. There's been a nasty flu going around and it'll help keep you healthy."

'Need everyone healthy. Healthy and happy.'

"Okay, I'll head there right now."

"Great. Oh, and did you find anything?"

"Not really. Everything's pretty much destroyed."

"I'm sorry, Sam. I really am."

"Me too."

I left before he could question me more, and headed to the clinic.

'Don't let them give you any drugs, Sam. Vitamins my ass.'

"I don't have a choice. There's nothing I can do about it."

He sighed mentally but didn't say anything more about it.

As I approached the clinic, Luke and Lucy walked past me. "Hey, where are you two going?"

They both smiled with glazed expressions that contained no hint of personality. "Just back to our room. See you around," Lucy said.

I couldn't hide my exasperation. What was going on? "Wait, what did you find out?"

Luke slugged my shoulder. "Oh, Sam, you worry too much. Everything's fine. They're waiting for you in there, and we have to go."

They walked away and left me stunned.

'Your friends have been compromised.'

"They're like pod people. I'm scared, Drake."

'Me too.'

But what could I do? I couldn't hide or escape, so I walked into the clinic and spied on every mind I could find, fighting a mounting headache the whole time.

***

My trepidation mounted when the doctor with the gold tooth walked into my room. "Hello, Sam." He flipped through a chart. "Looks like it's time for your vitamin dose. This is an enhanced version and will give you added health benefits as well as strengthen your powers."

"Who are you?"

"You are a direct young lady, aren't you? I'm Dr. Pana. I created this new serum and am overseeing the distribution of it."

'Sam, that's the doctor who treated me.'

"I know."

"Please hold out your arm and lie back. You might get dizzy or even fall asleep for a time. That's completely normal."

'Sam, don't! Please.'

"I have no choice."

My arm shook, but I offered it to him like a sacrificial lamb. For all my newfound courage, I still just let myself be pushed around. I'd never had any real power over my own life, and I realized I never would.

"Don't worry, it will only hurt for a second."

The prick came, and my body filled with a warm glow as I slid into oblivion.

Drake's voice touched at the edges of my consciousness. I reached for him, but he slipped farther and farther away, until he was gone and I was alone.

***

The little boy sits on the bed once again and waits. When New Daddy gets home, he's going to be ready for him this time.

New Mommy gets older every day and her skin wrinkles and sinks into itself in a yellowish muck. Drake won't hurt New Mommy, even if she does let New Daddy beat him.

New Mommy hurts herself enough for them both.

But New Daddy, he won't be allowed to do this anymore.

The door slams open and the little boy waits, quiet as a dead mouse.

Then New Daddy is standing over him, a gun in his hand.

The blow lands before Drake can move, but Drake's been practicing.

He pushes New Daddy's weak mind. He pushes harder and harder — with each bashing from the pistol, he pushes.

This beating hurts more than the rest. The metal from the gun breaks open his skin and bone. He might not heal from this, but he doesn't care as long as New Daddy doesn't either.

As Drake fades into darkness, as he becomes truly as quiet as a dead mouse — as a dead boy — he pushes one last time.

He hears the gunshot and feels New Daddy's brain and blood hit his face.

New Daddy shot himself.

***

The nightmare woke me from my drugged stupor. A deep ache built in my womb and pulsed through me. I calculated my cycle, but no, I still had a few weeks for that. Still the cramps burned inside me, as did the memory of that dream.

Of Drake's dream.

Drake's memories.

My breath hitched at the realization that all of my nightmares recently had been his. This was his childhood — his inner child, not mine.

I cried for him and called out to him in my mind.

'*I'm here. Are you okay?*'

"*Are you? I saw, Drake. I saw what happened to you.*"

He grew quiet and I feared he'd left.

'Do you hate me?'

"What? Why would I? You were a child trying to protect yourself. But what happened after your foster father killed himself?"

'I was in a coma for a week. Once I recovered, the orphanage took me back, and my foster mother was put on trial for abuse and negligence. I spent the next several years in and out of foster families until I finally ran away and moved in with my best friend Brad.'

My mind tumbled around as it tried to process what kind of life Drake must've had.

'How do you feel? You don't seem as drugged as your friends.'

"I don't feel that different. A little loopy and very achy."

I placed my hand on my abdomen. Sharp pain shot through me every few minutes. Maybe I had the flu. I did feel flushed. It could also be a side effect of this new "cocktail" they'd given me.

When Dr. Pana came into my room, I did my best impression of how Luke and Lucy had acted, and the doctor released me with instructions to rest for the remainder of the day.

If only a nice nap could have solved all my problems. I had to find a way to save my friends.

CHAPTER 13 – SAM

"Luke, Lucy, open up!" I rapped on their door again and tried the knob, as if it would magically unlock for me.

They'd never locked me out before.

Fear pricked my chest. I scanned for their mental signatures and reeled back in shock. Their minds had a weight and sluggishness to them that I'd never felt before.

My voice hitched with unshed tears. "Open up, please!"

Luke finally came to the door, and I hugged him hard. "What's wrong with you?"

"Don't know. Feel weird. Tired. Maybe we caught that flu."

I pushed my way in and felt his forehead. "You don't have a fever. Where's Lucy?"

"In bed sleeping."

I peeked in on her and then curled up on their couch. "Can I stay the night?"

Luke shrugged. "Whatever you want. I'm going to bed."

I wrapped myself in the throw blanket and reached out to Drake.

'I'm here.'

"I can't sleep."

'Neither can I. I'll stay up with you.'

And he did. When the sun came up, I finally fell asleep to the sound of his voice as he described Venice Beach.

The next morning, Luke and Lucy seemed less affected, but I woke up with a fever.

When I fell over while trying to stand, Luke picked me up and carried me back to the clinic. My weak protests did nothing to stop him.

"You're sick, Sam. Really sick. Like, 103-degree fever sick. You're going to the doctor."

I wanted to say, "The doctor that made me sick." Instead, I said something like, "Gumma mum ack," then threw up on Luke's chest and passed out.

***

I woke up groggy and in the Clinic. My head screamed at me to chop it off and put it out of its misery. My body clearly had been weighted down with lead.

"Good morning, sunshine." Dr. Sato, all five feet and ninety pounds of her, leaned in close.

Relief poured through me. Better her than Dr. Pana. "How long was I out? What happened to me?" My voice cracked, making me sound like a shipwreck survivor. I tried to lift my head. Bad idea. *Sorry head.*

"You get sick on boyfriend. He bring you here. You been unconscious. High fever."

"He's not my boyfriend." Mistrust tickled the back of my brain, and I instinctively reached for her mind to fill in the missing pieces of the story.

I'd been studying her dialect for weeks, but still hadn't learned enough to make sense of her thoughts.

A spasm in my abdomen wrenched me from her mind. I rested a hand on my stomach and tried to breathe.

"Are you all right? You hurting?"

"Just cramping. What am I sick with?"

"Likely flu. You be okay, just rest and fluids. Keep you here until you a little better."

I noticed the IV in my arm for the first time. "Can I go back to my room now?"

"Not yet. If you stay better and keep food down, you go to room and rest there."

"I am pretty hungry. Can I get something to eat?"

She nodded and left to get me lunch. Or dinner. I wasn't sure of the time.

After I downed a cold, limp turkey sandwich and green Jell-O, Dr. Sato declared me fit for bed rest in my own room. She unhooked me from the IV and went to sign me out.

My knees wobbled a bit as I began to dress, checking my body for anything abnormal. Nothing.

The walls kept me steady as I made my way through the Clinic. Just as the starch had returned to my legs....

'Sam! Sam! Where are you?'

"I'm here, at the clinic. I got sick. You feel so close. I want to be near you, in person, not just as a thought."

'Me too. Someday soon, I promise.'

I started following the sound of his thoughts, wandering through the halls, but the secure-password/scan-protected door stopped me short. Only certain staff members had clearance into that section of the Clinic.

But he was in there.

If anyone found out about this, I would be in trouble. But how would they know? They couldn't read my mind. Or could they? I put my hand on the forbidden door, trying to get closer to him. I needed to see him, to touch him and feel him.

'You shouldn't put yourself at risk. Don't get caught.'

"I just need to find you. Maybe I can get the drugs out of your system, and you can escape."

'Not without you. I'd never leave you here.'

My body melted against the door. I would have given anything in that moment to have Luke's powers. I could just walk through everything that stood between me and Drake.

"Sam, what are you doing here?" Dr. Sato stood behind me, fists on slight hips, glaring at me.

"I don't know. I'm sorry. I started feeling dizzy and got disoriented. I was just looking for a place to sit down." A simple lie made possible by a lifetime of acting.

Her composure softened. "You should have waited for the guard to escort you back to your room. Maybe you stay here is better."

She helped me up and guided me to her office. I sat down on her love seat, fighting waves of nausea but trying to hide it.

"Here. Drink."

I took the juice and drank greedily. My energy surged as the sugar hit my system.

I sighed and set the empty cup on the coffee table in front of me. "I'm feeling better. You said it's just the flu, right? My fever broke. There's no reason I can't recover in the comfort of my room."

"Yes, okay, but come back if you feel dizzy or nauseous, or if any other odd symptoms persist."

"I will."

She picked up her phone, and a moment later, a guard—*It's Gar!*—came in with a wheelchair. I groaned, just wanting to get home, but I felt better knowing Gar would be my escort.

***

Once we made it past prying ears I twisted to look at him. "Did you get demoted? This hardly seems a fitting job for one of your skill."

He didn't make eye contact with me. He didn't so much as twitch his face, but his voice hit my mind with force.

'I'm just here to keep you safe. That's my job.'

I pried deeper into his mind and saw that he had developed a soft spot for me after our assignment. It looked like I had my own guardian angel.

He dropped me at my dorm, walked me to my room, and then left without saying another word.

I dressed in my flannel pajamas and crawled into bed before I tried contacting Drake again.

On the one hand, a constant telepathic connection with him created a deep emotional intimacy. On the other hand, I needed him to be real and tangible, not just a voice.

"*Drake, can you hear me?*"

'Yes, what happened?'

I told him about my new friend and the trip back to my room. "*Want to see something?*"

'Sure.'

I'd been able to project the image of my painting to him; maybe I could do the same now. My tidy room, my closet with the door hanging open, the oak dresser and matching desk, a MacBook sitting on top of it—I imagined my mind as a computer, sending every captured image via email.

"*Can you see what I'm showing you?*" I didn't expect it to work. Vomiting and fevers didn't put me at my strongest.

'Is that your bedroom?'

"*Yes!*"

'It's nice. Cozy. Are those pictures of your friends on the wall?'

"Lucy and Luke, yes. And some other kids from class field trips."

'You're very pretty.'

"Thank you."

'Have you had a happy life here?'

Given his childhood memories, I could understand his curiosity. As bad as things had become, my life had been pretty good by comparison.

"That's tricky to answer. It's hard to miss what you never had, but when I read books, see TV shows or visit other families, I wonder what my life would have been like raised in a family. I guess I've always done my job knowing that when I turn eighteen, I'll be free to do what I want. I now have enough control not to put myself or others at risk. When I feel your visions, I know that my life has been pretty good compared to what you've endured."

'Your birthday's coming up, Sam. We need to talk about what happens next.'

I didn't know. So much had happened that I hadn't really given thought to my birthday and my release. College waited for me on the other side of this life, didn't it? Sarah Lawrence and freedom. But I knew—in the stillness of my heart I knew—it was all a dream of mist and vapors. It had never been real.

Mr. K's letter proved that. Other kids, they'd had going away parties. They'd been happy. We'd even gotten postcards from some of them.

I opened the bottom drawer of my nightstand and shuffled through some papers until I found what I needed. The Eifel Tower stood proud and glowing on the postcard, thousands of lights in the night. On the back, a postage stamp from Paris. *Hey, Sam, wish you were here. You'd love the Sorbonne. Stay good and enjoy your time in New York. Love, Rebekah.*

She'd been one of us. Now she was free. Or was she? Could it all have been faked? Would they really go through so much trouble to dupe us? If they had, then where were these kids? Where was Rebekah?

I projected my thoughts and the image of the postcard to Drake. I told him the story we'd been fed our whole lives—that Rent-A-Kid kept us safe, trained us and prepared us for the real world. Our parents had given us up to protect us.

'Sam, you know too much. Did all your parents give you up willingly? Why weren't they involved in your lives at all? Have any ever come to visit or interact with their kids? You don't think those postcards can be forged?'

"Our parents gave us up because they couldn't handle kids like us. They did what was best for us." It was true. It had to be true. I needed it to be true.

'Then why couldn't they at least stay in touch? Visit? Call?'

"I don't know. Probably for safety. We get to meet our families when we leave. Once we are safe."

'You keep talking about being safe, but they have rented you out since you were thirteen. You've been safe enough for clients for a long time, so why not let your family back into your life? Come on, Sam, you're a smart girl, but they've got you brainwashed to believe they are the good guys. They are not the good guys. They tracked me down, attacked me, and brought me here against my will. You and I both know they weren't saving me from anyone. Does that sound like something a good organization would do?'

My head pounded, the pain coming back full force, and I didn't want to deal with these questions.

I would figure it out later. "Drake, I admit that something isn't right here. At the very least, Dr. Pana is a problem, and someone's stealing powers, but that doesn't mean everything has been a lie. Look, I've been sick, and I'm crashing. Can we talk later?"

'Okay. Hey Sam....'

"Hmm?"

'Be careful.'

That night, stolen kids and heartbroken parents filled my dreams. I woke up more exhausted than when I'd fallen asleep, drenched in sweat, my heart racing.

CHAPTER 14 – SAM

Two days of forced bed rest left little room for fun.

After reading the first three chapters of every book in my possession, and countless hours studying Dr. Sato's dialect, I needed reinforcements.

Poor Drake had already put up with so much. *"You must be so sick of my whining and moping and all my Japanese thinking. I'm sorry. I'm just so bored!"*

'I'm not sick of you, and I can relate. I'm strapped down to a bed and powerless, after all. By the way, you're a freaking genius with language. I can't believe how much you've learned in just three days. How do you do it? I barely know Spanish and I grew up surrounded by it.'

His praise released a flutter of butterflies in my stomach. Learning languages and reading minds wasn't nearly as exciting as hacking computers, walking through walls or kicking butts in martial arts. I loved that he thought my gifts were special.

"I've been studying languages since I was two years old. It's always come naturally."

'*How many can you speak?*'

I had to do the math in my head. *"Um, thirty or so, plus a few dialects."*

'*Holy crap! That's seriously impressive. When we get out of this mess, we totally have to travel all over the world. You'll be able to talk to everyone.*'

My heart swelled with images of walking hand-in-hand with Drake through the streets of Italy, touring the great cathedrals in France, eating at a café and chatting with the locals.... But the best part—visiting all the greatest museums of the world. What I wouldn't give to spend hours at the Louvre and the Rodin museum in France, the Van Gough Museum in Amsterdam, the Los Angeles County Museum of Art, the New York Metropolitan Museum of Art.... My mind trailed off into the lands of the greatest artists, and I "showed" Drake memories of my favorite paintings throughout history.

As soon as class got out, Lucy and Luke came over bearing gifts—flowers, a get well card, chicken soup, and a new DVD.

"You guys, I'm not dying. It's just a bad flu." I acted annoyed but appreciated the kindness.

Lucy handed me the soup and a spoon. "I know, Chica, but we figured you were bored out of your mind, and this might cheer you up."

I smiled. "It has."

Luke sat in my favorite chair, his long legs spread out before him. Lucy sat at the edge of my bed. They both seemed happy enough, but still not quite right. Their eyes looked glazed over, and they had an artificial calm to them.

"So spill it, what's going on with you and Drake?" Lucy asked.

"Nothing." I tried to look innocent as I sipped my soup.

"Nope. Try again."

I put the soup down and switched to our made-up language. "Don't you guys find it odd that we all got sick after our recent 'vitamin' injections?"

Lucy's eyes fogged over, then cleared. "I feel fine, Sam. I don't know what you're talking about."

I looked to Luke for support. "You both were like zombies, and then I came down with this flu. And now you seem... different. Less suspicious."

Luke smiled, but with a shadow of his normal brightness. "Lighten up, Sam. Life's too short to worry so much."

I cried out to Drake in frustration. *"What do I do?"*

'Maybe if we work together, we can push them to remember. Help clear their minds.'

"It's worth a try, I guess. Okay, you stay with me while I link to them. Instead of pulling their thoughts from them, I'll try to push my thoughts into them."

Messing with my best friends' minds made me nervous, but so did their way-too-carefree new personalities.

With Drake in tow, I focused on Luke first. Once again, a haze of heaviness settled on me and lured me to sleep, but Drake's mental tether kept me alert. I imagined the haze lifting and clarity returning. I pushed my will into the thought and felt Drake do the same. Almost immediately, my link weakened as the amount of power it took to create this level of connection drained me. After being so sick, I had very little energy left, but I couldn't give up.

It worked. With one last push, Luke's mind regained some of its former energy.

We pulled out and did the same with Lucy.

When we were done, I closed my eyes and wiped away the tears that slid down my cheek. I'd never felt more exhausted in my life.

Luke's voice had more energy than before. "You okay, Sam? What did you do? I feel like I just woke up from sleepwalking."

Without opening my eyes, I answered him. "Do you remember the shot the doctor gave you? Being sick?"

Lucy's voice joined the conversation. "Yes, I do now. Damn, I'm so sorry we doubted you. It's weird. Part of me still thinks everything is okay and I should just chill out, and another part feels a panic at what's happening.

My friends were back.

"Thank you, Drake."

'I'm glad it worked.'

Now that they could think for themselves, it was time to talk about our future.

***

"Do either of you wonder about our parents?"

Luke's face hardened. He and Lucy had been left by their parents at a hospital as babies. Rent-A-Kid somehow got to them before Social Services could intervene. "Not really. It's better that way."

With the residual mental link to Luke still active, flashes of memory fluttered into my mind: A woman with large brown eyes and a soft smile humming a lullaby and rocking him and Lucy.

Their mother.

I looked to Luke, but he didn't make eye contact, so I pushed it aside and continued our conversation.

"But if my parents were just doing what was best for me, then why haven't they been allowed to visit? Why don't any of us have contact with them? What if... what if they didn't give us up willingly?"

Lucy stiffened. "Where is this coming from, Sam?"

I kept my voice calm and reasonable. "As you said yourself, Higgins lied to you. Someone stole Kyle's powers and sabotaged my art project. Mr. K disappeared, and now they've drugged us. Our future may not be as secure as we'd hoped. What if we aren't released and let into the world when we turn eighteen?"

Lucy's voice sounded hollow as she spoke. "I just can't bring myself to believe that it's not true, Sam. Why don't we just focus on one problem at a time? We have to figure out what happened to your painting."

I suppose we all were desperate to believe, because to doubt the truth of this place meant questioning everything about our lives. Exploring the alternatives made my stomach clench worse than this flu. We were nearly eighteen, and Drake's ideas left me unsettled and fearful of my future. I wanted to let it go, to just stick to the current problem, but my birthday was fast approaching. Suddenly, the loss of my painting paled in comparison to these new problems.

"You guys, Drake made some good points, things we'd have thought of already if we weren't too scared to face the truth. Why have they taken him and locked him up? If they were really saving him from a threat, why haven't they released him? And why don't we have any contact with the outside world except on assignment?"

"It's for our protection," Luke straightened in the chair, his muscles tense. "If they knew what we could do, we would be locked up and tested like a bunch of lab rats."

"I don't buy it. By the time we were old enough for assignments, we were old enough to keep our own secrets and control our powers. So what secret are they keeping from us?"

"I can tell when people are lying," said Lucy. "Don't you think I would know if there was a big conspiracy?"

True. We called Lucy our human lie detector. And I could read minds, so how could they keep the truth from us? What would be the easiest way—

Of course. "They aren't lying!"

"That's what we're saying." Luke slumped back in the chair, a smirk on his face.

"No! I mean, what if they only tell the people we have contact with the cover story, not the truth? So those people aren't actually lying. After all, this organization is bigger than we know. We've never even met the people at the top. Maybe our teachers and the staff really believe we'll leave to our new life when we turn eighteen. And besides, Lucy, you said Higgins lied about Mr. K. Something is clearly going on!"

Their crestfallen faces evaporated my enthusiasm.

"Oh, my God, Sam," Lucy said. "What if you're right? What if we don't really get to leave? What do they do with us then?"

Luke's fist balled. "Lucy, don't encourage her. This is all bullshit."

I ignored him. "Drake was right about one thing: we know too many secrets. We'd be too dangerous in the world on our own. Even if we don't know the location of this property, we know where our assignments have been. We know the dirty secrets of some of the richest, most powerful people in the world. How could they take the chance of letting us go free? Think about it!"

We sat there, staring at nothing, lost in our own dark thoughts. Before they could object more, I showed them the letter Mr. K had left me.

"Mr. K suspected something, then he

disappeared."

"So what do we do?" Luke asked. "If you're right, or if your boyfriend is right—What do we do? We don't know what happens when kids leave here. We don't know anyone on the outside, and we've no way of contacting them if we did. This place is impossible to escape from. I'm not saying we just give up, but we need a plan."

"Does that mean you believe me?" If I had to face the truth, I wanted my best friends with me, as selfish as that sounded.

"I'm not sure, but you have a point. We'd be stupid not to think about it. But without any outside connections, we're dead in the water." He stared out the window, lost in his own thoughts.

"*We* may not know anyone, but Drake does. His best friend is a reporter in California, maybe he can help."

"*Drake, what do you think?*"

'*Brad's probably freaking out right now. I know he'd do anything to help us, but we need a way of contacting him. He's going to give me such shit for not listening to him earlier.*'

"*What could you do? You can't live in fear and you can't ever give up on your dreams. If you do, they win and you're trapped even if free. You did the right thing. It's what I would have done.*"

That may not have been true before. I hadn't always had the courage to do what was in my heart, despite pressure or fear, but I knew in that moment I had changed in some indefinable and permanent way. Whoever I'd been, I now possessed a determination that couldn't be undone by the unknown.

I shared Drake's idea with Lucy and Luke.

"That sounds like a possibility," Luke said, "but how would we get ahold of this guy? Not like we get free access to the outside world."

I thought about it. "I'm supposed to be going on another assignment soon—with Mary."

"What about your guard?" Luke asked.

"He doesn't follow me to the bathroom. If I get Brad's phone number from Drake, and steal someone's cell phone for a few minutes, maybe I can make a call."

Lucy nibbled on her lower lip. "That might work, but you'd have to be really careful."

I rolled my eyes. "No, I thought I'd announce my plan to everyone!"

"Don't be a smartass, Chica, this could be really dangerous."

"I can't think of anything else. Can you? We're too isolated here. We have no other choice."

We stared at one another, and each of us nodded in turn. No one really expected a better plan to land in our laps.

***

Lucy and Luke saw me before anyone else the next day, and tag-teamed hugged me.

"You're off the deathbed, and you don't look like a sexy ghost anymore," said Lucy. "I knew the soup we brought would make you better!"

"Yes, I'm sure that's exactly what did it." I always looked pale compared to them.

We got to our English class and settled into our seats in the back. I mentally checked everyone, but it was just more of the usual—boys, girls, parties, tests, fear of the future, excited or nervous about the next assignment.

Peter, a boy who'd been asking me out for a few years, sent a papier-mâché rose floating through the air to my desk. His attention had never ignited the same fire in me that my connection with Drake had. A surge of jealousy rose up from Drake, who sat in my mind like a split personality—so much a part of me now, it was hard to tell where my mind stopped and his started. I assured him that Peter held no interest for me. Our teacher, Mr. Jackson, glared at Peter and nodded to me, the only indication he'd give that I'd been out sick. Fine by me.

"We are discussing Macbeth: the symbolism, the misogyny, and the thematic elements that have made this play so popular over the years." When Mr. Jackson lectured, it was as if he did so from a stage, and I wondered idly if he had a background in theater. "Who can tell me about one of the most significant symbols in Macbeth. Sam?"

I hadn't even raised my hand! But that's what I got for missing class. I flipped through my edition of the famous Scottish play and looked at the notes I'd taken for my essay.

"Blood. Blood is everywhere in Macbeth. The opening battle between the Scots and the Norwegian invaders in Act 1 is very bloody. And once Macbeth and Lady Macbeth start killing everyone, it holds significant symbolism for them both.

"After Macbeth kills Duncan, he talks about Neptune's ocean washing away this blood from his hand, and later, when Lady Macbeth falls to her conscience, she gets obsessive about trying to clean her hands of the blood. Blood symbolizes the guilt that sits like a permanent stain on the consciences of both Macbeth and Lady Macbeth, one that hounds them to their graves."

Mr. Jackson clapped. "Very good, Sam. I take it that is the theme of your essay."

"Yes."

"Wonderful. Now, on to misogyny. Why do you think so many people have accused Shakespeare of hating women?"

My mind wandered, and I pulled out my new sketchbook and placed it over Macbeth. The leather felt smooth under my palm as I flipped through the pages I'd filled—a portrait of Tommy playing with his truck, his youthful smile so contagious; several pages of Drake, or what I imagined he would look like if standing or sitting, rather than lying on a gurney; even a portrait of Mr. K, hawk nose and all.

A renegade tear threatened to ruin my composition, but I caught it before it could fall. *Will I ever see Mr. K again?*

Dozens of sketches of the twins covered the pages. Over the years, I'd painted, sketched, or in some way drawn nearly every inch of this place, including the entire faculty and every student. My secret notebooks proved that I'd really been here.

Even if just to myself.

CHAPTER 15 – SAM

Over the next few weeks, dizziness and nausea thwarted my plans to help Drake or learn anything new. My illness forced me to leave class twice to go to the Clinic. This continued despite the fact that my face had healed well, and the flu shouldn't last that long.

With my eighteenth birthday days away, I still hadn't heard from Higgins about my next assignment. This would be my last chance to get off campus and get us some help.

In addition to losing all excitement for my future, my concern for Drake buzzed in my mind like a pestering bee. As his strength faded by the day, he became more and more ill.

'Sam!'

My history professor enlightened us about some war or another. I pretended to pay attention while listening to Drake.

'I heard the nurses talking. They're moving me, but I don't know where.'

My heart skipped a beat, but I forced myself to stay calm and keep up appearances. *"I don't know what to do. I haven't figured out anything."*

'They're coming in. Sam!'

"Drake! Drake!"

Nothing.

I ran out of the classroom, startling everyone next to me, and headed to the nearest bathroom. *"Drake. Drake!"*

He didn't answer. They'd probably drugged him unconscious.

I fought in vain to keep tears from spilling down my cheeks. The bathroom door opened and Lucy walked in. I splashed water on my face to wipe away any evidence, and dried off, hands still shaking, heart still racing.

"Sam, are you okay?"

The flood gates opened again, and I told Lucy everything.

"Oh, Chica, I'm so sorry. We'll sort it out." She held me as I cried into her shoulder.

Then my stomach rumbled, and I threw myself at the nearest stall, just barely making it to the toilet before practically puking up my intestines.

"Is she okay?"

Great, Luke was there too. Sometimes his ability to walk through walls unnerved everyone around him. The heaving stopped. I wiped my mouth with toilet paper and stood up slowly.

Lucy protested. "Luke, this is the girl's room, you're not allowed in here! Just... never mind. Help her."

"Sam, no arguments." He put a little extra thunder in his voice. "I'm taking you to the Clinic, again. You know, I should start charging you a service fee as a personal escort."

Lucy scowled at him. "Luke, grow up."

I stumbled out to the sink and rinsed my face and mouth. The sight of my skin, like paste dotted in beads of sweat, made me feel even worse.

***

They escorted me through the halls. Luke kept a hand on my shoulder, in case I got a bit too wobbly.

Lucy said, "I already told Mr. Vecarali that I'd make sure you got to the Clinic. He gave us all passes."

On the way there, Lucy filled Luke in on what had happened to Drake.

"While we're in there, Sam, try to ferret anything you can from the staff's minds. Lucy, you ask some questions, see if anyone is lying. Sam said Missy knew something, so ask her. I'll see if I can discreetly slip through a few locked doors and find anything."

The twins left me in the care of Dr. Sato and went to do their spying. I tried to make contact with Drake but still couldn't reach him. What if they'd already moved him somewhere too far away? What if they'd hurt him? And as always, my mind kept coming back to the same questions. Why? Why bring him in now? They couldn't rent him out, because he was a loose cannon—but he wasn't a true danger. So what use did they have for him?

And what would they do to me when I turned eighteen? These days, my grief over my art had been replaced by fear for my life. What a change a few months could make.

I clutched my stomach as another spasm rode me. Dr. Sato rushed to my side and led me to a bed. While she helped me change into a hospital gown, I tried to scan her thoughts.

My language skills had improved enough that the dialect wasn't too hard to understand now. Still, people usually don't think in coherent sentences, which made context very important.

'She's sick... hope baby okay... color... yellow... the boy is trouble... but strong powers... their baby is good... fear... I want....'

I didn't know what to make of it all. What baby? What was she talking about? As I reclined on the bed, she got out an ultrasound machine.

"I check your belly for sickness," she told me, her English more broken than normal.

'Shouldn't feel it yet... can't let her see....'

Can't let me see what?

She hid the screen from me as she squirted my abdomen with cold jelly and rubbed the camera over it.

'Baby too big... growing too fast... definitely pregnant.'

"Pregnant?" I spoke out loud before thinking.

She flinched. Only slightly, but enough that I knew I had hit the mark.

"Where you hear about pregnant? I not pregnant," she said, clearly trying to deflect the conversation.

'This girl reading mind?... never reads mine... what tell them?'

Her thoughts froze me. What the hell? I couldn't be pregnant. I'd never even had sex! It's not that I had anything against sex, but when your every move is watched and recorded, it kinda takes the romance out of it. Besides, I'd never met a guy I was really into until....

Oh, my God. Drake, a boy I hadn't even met in person yet, had already taken over my thoughts and my heart. I needed him. And he needed me. Where was he?

"Drake?" Still nothing.

He'd been a part of my waking and sleeping consciousness for months. With him gone, so completely gone that even his trace mental signature didn't register, I felt like an empty vessel. A terrifying loneliness and fear gripped me.

My head swam with conflicting realities.

This couldn't be happening. This wasn't real. I must have misunderstood her Japanese. For nearly two months I'd spent every spare moment I could studying her dialect, but there was so much to learn. I probably misinterpreted the entire thing and panicked for nothing.

Logically, this made sense, but my body knew the truth. Even as I denied it, I could feel the new life growing inside me.

And suddenly my being pregnant made a horrible kind of sense.

They needed more kids. If we were right, and they basically ran a paranormal human trafficking ring, they needed as many of us as they could get. And what better way to get more paranormals than to breed them? Is that why they'd gotten rid of Mr. K? Had he come too close to the truth? Is that why they'd burned down the art studio? Of course, I could never succeed in public. They never meant for me to have an art career or go to Sarah Lawrence.

Dr. Sato glanced over her shoulder at me as she left the room, closed the door and.... Did she lock it? Oh crap!

I scanned all the minds in the Clinic that I could find. Missy talked with Lucy. She was nervous, lying, thinking about Drake. He'd been moved to another facility. They'd gotten what they needed from him, but she didn't know what that was. She'd overheard something she shouldn't have, and it scared her.

I searched for Luke. I usually stayed out of my friends' minds, out of respect. No one wants to be best friends with someone who is always spying on their thoughts. But I didn't think he'd mind me sneaking a peek under the circumstances.

I found him. His mind sorted through information, breaking into fragments—worried about getting caught, looking at records. My records.

'Sam is pregnant?... what?... what the hell have they done to her?... oh my God... Drake... that's why they took him... wanted his powers to breed with... Oh Sam... how will I tell her?... what are we going to do?... oh shit... Lucy... she'll be eighteen soon... sons of bitches... I'm going to kill them all....'

I stopped listening, paralyzed. It was true. I was pregnant, and it looked like Drake was the father.

CHAPTER 16 – SAM

Dr. Sato didn't release me from the Clinic. My door remained locked, and she alone came and went. She said I had a dangerous stomach virus that could make others sick, but to which she was immune. Yeah right.

I celebrated my eighteenth birthday with her and the few books she allowed to occupy my time. They bored me to death.

Worrying about Drake made me sick, as no one had any useful information. Missy had been mysteriously replaced by a new receptionist who knew nothing relevant.

Lucy and Luke's thoughts revealed their desperate need to reach me, but I couldn't communicate with them like I could with Drake. That still puzzled me.

Dr. Sato did allow me to keep notebooks, so I started writing everything I wanted to say to Drake in my special language. That journal became my only connection to him, or anyone else, for three long weeks.

The torture of isolation, of endless contemplation, forced me to analyze every detail of my existence at Rent-A-Kid. We often got postcards from kids who had left to start their new life, and I got care packages from my "parents." They could easily fake these, use them to keep us passive and hopeful, and from rocking the boat or questioning our lives.

It had worked.

How could I have been so gullible for so long? I had allowed myself to become the ultimate victim in every area of my life, from the Rent-A-Kid nightmare to the bullies at school or on assignment.

And what about my life goals—if I ever got to have a real life? My teachers always encouraged me to pursue linguistics and to do something with international relations. That made sense, but really, once I left here, I wanted to get as far away from this life as possible.

My life up until now had been pretty shallow. And now, just as I saw the truth, they locked me up and made me impotent. Rent-A-Kid turned me into a victim once again, unable to affect any kind of change.

Each time my mind turned toward the baby growing in my stomach, an intense and overwhelming panic took over, until I couldn't think or focus. My heart rate would skyrocket, and Dr. Sato would come in with something in a syringe that put me to sleep.

The utter betrayal and violation of having my body raped without my knowledge.... I had no way of processing this level of terror.

My purgatory ended on a day as boring as the rest, when Dr. Sato came in smiling.

"Good news. Your tests are clear and you can go. You have party waiting and friends. Then you go to New York."

"Wait, I was supposed to have another assignment before I left." I needed that assignment to connect with Brad.

"That canceled. You too sick. But okay for party."

I couldn't believe my ears, so I listened with my mind. *'Can't... disappear... friends miss her... must do party... not showing yet... must move her....'*

So they would move me. But where? If only I had Drake's ability to control other people. How did he do that? And how did they catch a streetwise, super-strong guy who could control people? How had they even found him? If they could contain him, my chances of escape seemed pretty slim.

I instinctively put a hand over my abdomen; it happened a lot these days. I moved it before Dr. Sato noticed. The reasons to resent this child, this pregnancy, grew daily. Yet love grew in my heart despite it all. This baby could not be blamed for the way in which it had been conceived, and it was my job to protect it. From them. From the world.

Even the horror of its inception could not keep me from loving what Drake and I had created.

What would Drake say when he found out? If he found out? If he'd served his purpose, what would they do to him? Would they just... get rid of him? I doubted they'd let him go, but my mind refused to consider the alternative.

Dr. Sato handed me a beautiful red ball gown. It was to be a fancy affair, my fake going-away party. After a quick shower, I did up my long hair in a French twist, put on makeup and jewelry from the supplies Dr. Sato handed me, and slipped on my red heels. I was ready to make my entrance.

And my exit.

***

When Lucy and Luke saw me outside the ballroom entrance, they nearly plowed me over with hugs.

"What happened to you?" "We tried to visit but they wouldn't let us in." "Are you okay?" "We have so much to tell you."

"Wow, hold on a sec guys, one at a time. I have a confession to make. I've been spying on you. I know it goes against our friendship code, but I was so anxious to know what was happening."

Luke looked so sad it nearly made me cry. "So you know?" He reached for my hand.

I switched to our special language. "Yes, I know about the baby and about Drake."

They hugged me again—the way friends hug when words just aren't enough.

"We can talk, but we have to pretend like we're celebrating. We can't let them know we know, and we obviously need a new plan. Apparently, I won't be going on that last assignment."

They nodded and, each holding one of my hands, my best friends gave me the strength to play the role of the happy girl heading to Sarah Lawrence.

All of my training did not prepare me for this hardest of parts. My heart broke with each smile. Unshed tears crushed my soul. I mourned the end of my dreams even as a fake smile greeted my small world.

I left the cool stillness of the night and walked into my going-away party. The onslaught of sounds, smells and colors sent my head spinning for a moment. I paused, taking in the scene of happy teenagers talking, laughing, eating.

They all still lived in the bubble created for us. Only we three knew the truth. How would we save ourselves from this? And what would become of them?

Amidst the crowd of school friends, a guard shadowed me. I relaxed at the sight of Gar. He gave the briefest of nods, so slight I could have imagined it, and then he turned back to stone.

"That's new," Luke said, glancing at Gar.

"Yeah. Wonder why they felt he was necessary. But, at least they sent a guard I trust." I hoped I hadn't given away something when I commented about the pregnancy to Dr. Sato. Did they suspect me of knowing too much?

Lucy nudged me. "Don't let it bother you, Chica. Try to have fun!"

I forced a smile back onto my face. "You're right. Why not enjoy it?"

The campus actually had a full-fledged ballroom, not just a gym they converted once a year for dances. We learned ballroom, swing, and modern dancing as part of our education. Parties at our school were high-end affairs.

Scarlet red and royal purple silks draped the room. Lush roses accented the hall and served as centerpieces in crystal vases on the tables. A full band played music suited to dancing in many diverse styles, and students already swayed across the room in long trailing dresses and elegant tuxes.

My mind searched for Drake, the way a woman might reach for her lover across an empty bed. If he'd been here, we would have been one of those couples on the dance floor. His arms would have wrapped around me, encircling me in a cocoon of love and safety. I might have brushed my hand against his chiseled jawline, and maybe he'd have leaned down and brush his lips against mine for a first kiss.

The fantasy played around me and replaced my reality for just a moment. Then the bubble burst and I once again stood alone in a sea of oblivion.

"Sam, come on, let's get some food." Lucy and Luke pulled me to the buffet table.

A dozen well-wishers interrupted us on our way there: Greg and Gary, a new couple I only knew in passing; Kyle, who looked dejected and guilty, despite my best attempts to absolve him; Norm and Robyn, another couple who'd been together for as long as I could remember... and so many others. The gift table overflowed with cards and special trinkets from friends. I complimented Robyn on her emerald dress that matched her eyes, and told Norm he was a lucky guy. They smiled and moved onto the dance floor.

Only a handful of kids had left Rent-A-Kid so far. We were first generation paranormals. No one knew how we got our powers, but I was one of the oldest. Kids made a big deal out of these parties, even if they didn't know the person who left. It was the gift of hope, the promise of a future outside these chained grounds. No one missed a going-away party.

It took us a while to navigate through all of our friends and make it to the food, but the spread of goodies made our trek well worth it. The table overflowed with mouthwatering delicacies. I reached to stuff a truffle into my mouth, but my stomach rebelled stubbornly at the smell. Damn pregnancy. I nibbled at some crab rolls instead, to appease my friends. I stole glances at the delicious treats, wishing on this miserable night that I could at least enjoy the chocolate.

Everyone danced. One guy hovered off the ground while he moved to the music, doing breakdancing moves in the sky, but he fell to the ground when his date suddenly burst into flames. Jessica, who'd been cooling drinks for her friends, blew on the girl to subdue the flames. The crowd erupted in applause—except Mary, who'd snuck off with the breakdancing boy during all the commotion. I'd lost track of how many dates she had stolen from other girls that night. Typical paranormal party.

We endured another hour of snacking, talking and pretending, and I was almost enjoying myself when Mary sashayed toward us, wearing a gorgeous black dress that left her shoulders bare and hugged her chest and hips in all the right places. Her blond hair fell in ringlets down her back.

She puckered her lips at Luke and moved in a way that revealed her well-toned thigh and ample cleavage. Luke ignored her. I hid a smile.

Mary scowled and looked at me. "Sam, you're back. We've missed you. Are you feeling well?"

Did she really care? I kept my answers brief. "I'm fine, thank you."

"I hear you're heading off to Sarah Lawrence soon. You must be so excited."

Did she know something? Why the change of attitude? Niceness and Mary didn't go together, and I didn't trust it at all.

But, regretting my behavior in the bathroom so long ago, I tried to play nice too. "Yes, it'll be quite an adventure."

"Well, be sure to keep in touch." She walked away before I could reply that I would. Her shallow mind mused about the hottest boys in school. *'Gotta get my hands on Luke... how can he resist me?'*

I chuckled at that.

Lucy pulled me away and demanded my attention. She stole the night in an electric blue gown that wrapped itself around her slim figure like saran wrap. Luke had matched his bowtie to her gown, completing the look. They made an unforgettable pair.

"Looks like Mary finally learned her lesson after the cafeteria and bathroom scenes. It's about time."

Before I could reply, an achingly familiar voice interrupted my thoughts.

'Sam, can you hear me?'

"Drake! Oh, my God, I've missed you. What happened? Where are you?"

'In another hospital. I don't know where. I've been trying to talk to you, but you haven't replied.'

In my hospital, they'd given me an IV. Could it have been something to control my powers? I could still read Dr. Sato's mind, and kids on campus, but maybe it prevented me from linking long distance.

"I think they did something to me so I couldn't talk to you. I'm out of the hospital now, but I'm at my going-away party. I'm supposed to be leaving for New York tomorrow."

'You were in the hospital? What happened? Are you okay?'

He had no idea about what I'd been through or that I was pregnant. What to tell him? Ahh... I so did not want to have this conversation.

My hand went to my stomach again.

"Sam, you okay? You look pale. Come sit down." Luke guided me to a chair and Lucy brought me some punch. Gar hovered nearby, trying without success to blend in.

"Hey. I have to talk to my friends for a minute."

'Sure.'

I spoke in our language. "Drake's okay. He's in some hospital. But I... I have to tell him about the baby."

They nodded sympathetically and watched over me while I linked back to Drake. "I need to talk to you about something, but I don't know how to say it."

'What's wrong? Are you okay?'

What could I do? I just blurted it out. *"I'm pregnant. And it looks like you're the father."*

And that is how I turned the whole world quiet for a moment. Drake sat in mental silence. Luke and Lucy looked heartbroken. And the rest of the world disappeared.

Drake broke the silence first.

"I believe you. And I think you're right. I think they're... um... harvesting me for reproductive purposes."

Despite how horrible everything seemed, I couldn't help but laugh out loud at his choice of words, at how proper he was trying to be. Lucy and Luke eyed me curiously. I explained what Drake had said. Lucy smirked, and Luke laughed.

I sobered up pretty quickly, though. How could he be so certain? *"What did they do to you?"*

'I can just tell that things were done to... parts of me. I didn't know what to make of it until now. How do you know you're pregnant though? They didn't tell you, did they?'

"No, but I overheard some of the doctor's thoughts. And Luke saw the records. That's why they took you. You have incredibly strong and rare para-powers. And I can tell. My body is different."

Luke and Lucy interrupted our conversation with a glance over my shoulder. I turned to look.

My bodyguard headed our way. "Is everything okay?"

I smiled as sweetly as I could. "Of course! Just tired from all the partying."

Gar nodded and walked back to stand in my shadow.

He may have been committed to protecting me, but he still worked for them.

***

The night crawled on. After the formal dancing, the music picked up and included songs our age group actually knew. I declined all offers to dance, instead spending my time with Lucy, Luke and Drake. His presence was like finding a fresh water lake in the middle of the desert. I couldn't get enough of his voice, his thoughts, the weight of his mind in mine.

My headaches had become less severe the more I practiced remote linking. My powers were getting stronger, more controlled. Before, everyone's thoughts inundated me, but now I could tune out people selectively. Such a relief from all the inane clattering. Most people didn't understand, bombarded with their own thoughts, unable to find peace in even that. To have that multiplied by everyone around me was hell. And people generally weren't very interesting. Most of their thoughts were recycled, replaying on an endless loop.

My appetite improved halfway through the party, and I ate a little bit of everything on the table, finally satiating my craving for chocolate.

The party wound down after 1 AM. All of our friends said their goodbyes and wished me luck. Envy and hope surfaced in their eyes. Everyone yearned for the time when they could be free to live the life of their choosing.

For a moment, I longed for the false peace that accompanied their ignorance. They all had such hope—the hope I tore from my closest friends, who now had to stay here knowing that their future would not be the one promised. I pushed away the twinge of guilt that crept into my heart. They needed to know. I needed to know. We couldn't escape the truth by remaining blind to it. Now that the truth had been forced on us, maybe we could find a way out of this mess.

What would they do to me once the baby was born? Would they keep using my body for more and more pregnancies, until I became a useless shell? Then what? Kill me? Being a Rent-A-Kid prisoner seemed a much better life compared to a future as a baby factory, all the while knowing that my children were here, rented out like property, awaiting the same fate as me.

I couldn't let that happen. I wouldn't let that happen.

'Neither will I,' Drake said.

We arrived at my room with Gar right behind us. Would I be locked in tonight to keep me from trying to escape?

Where would I go? How would I save Drake? I had too many questions, no answers, and no idea what to do.

Lucy and Luke came in, and we all sat on my bed, with me in the middle. I lived in the manner in which my many personas would have expected to live: in luxury. No doubt, my new quarters would not be this fine. After all, my new role didn't require me to be comfortable and at ease in wealth, did it? I just had to ovulate properly.

"What do we do?" I spoke out loud in our made-up language, but English in my mind. Confusing, but I didn't know who might be spying on us.

"You should try to escape tonight," Luke said. "We could help you get out. There's a fence by the north field that had a short last night. We could get through that."

"You don't think they're monitoring those too? And what about the brick walls past the fence? And whatever is beyond that? And the guards, and the trackers in our arms?"

Lucy fought tears. "You can't let them take you, Sam."

My body numbed. "What else can I do right now? We can't escape with so many people watching. And I can't leave Drake, wherever he is. They'll probably put us in the same facility, right? I mean, if they're using him to breed, then we should be able to find each other. Maybe we can escape from there, and then we can get help for you guys."

'I will do everything I can to get us out of here, Sam. I swear it. I need to get off these drugs, and I think I know

a way. If you're brought here, you can help. We can do this. But if there's any way for you to escape before getting here, you have to take it!'

"I'm not leaving you alone there. I'll find a way to get us both out, and we'll find a way to save the rest."

"I have to go. I have to get evidence of what's happening here." I scooted off the bed and went to my backpack. Inside, hidden in a secret pouch, lay a tiny camera. I'd kept it out of impulse, though it was against rules.

I palmed it and brought it back to the bed with me. "Look discreetly at my hand. I have a camera that I stole from my last job."

Luke's eyes widened. "You stole a camera?"

I nodded. "It has pictures of me and Tommy on it. I gave him the pictures I had, and I just wanted to keep these."

"How were you ever planning on developing them?" Lucy asked.

"I wasn't thinking about all of that. I just had to have something to prove I knew him."

Lucy sighed. "So you want us to take pictures of this place?"

"Yes, I have artwork depicting everything and everyone here, but I doubt that will count as hard evidence. Especially get pictures of the kids with obvious para-powers."

Luke scratched his head. "Assuming we can get those pictures without getting caught, what would we do with them?"

"We need to find a way of getting this to Drake's friend." I gave them Brad's email and phone number, and handed Luke the camera. "Get this to him. Tell him everything we've told you and everything you've experienced. At least someone on the outside will know that we exist and need help."

A knock at the door startled us all. Luke slipped the camera into his pocket.

The door opened. "It's time to go," Gar said to me.

"I thought I was leaving in the morning?" Panic rose in my chest. This was too real, too fast.

'Relax, we'll find a way to get out.'

I wondered what it would be like to meet Drake in person. He filled my imagination—his voice, his scent, the feel of his skin. He'd taken up residence inside my body, somehow. Would that change when we really could touch, when I could actually smell him and feel him for real?

"Plans changed. Get your stuff and say goodbye." He grabbed two of my biggest bags. I picked up my backpack and a small suitcase—all of my worldly belongings. Apparently, they'd packed everything while I was in the hospital. How thoughtful.

I checked my backpack to make sure my sketch pad and the box from Mr. K were still there. I'd kept the cash I'd earned from assignments in Mr. K's secret compartment. That would come in handy if we found a way to escape.

Lucy's tears finally fell. Even Luke's eyes watered. From the time we were little, we'd only been apart during assignments. Now we might never see each other again.

I hugged them both, then threw on my jean jacket and backpack, and walked out of my room for what would likely be the last time.

Gar closed the door, and Luke and Lucy, behind us.

I turned to him as we walked down the hall. "Don't I even get a chance to change my clothes?" I wiped my eyes carefully to avoid the makeup raccoon look.

"You can change when you get to your new home. Your flight was changed. We leave now."

Could Gar know what fate he was leading me to? I slipped into his mind.

'She'll be safe in New York... will make sure she's looked after... finally out of here....'

He had no idea. At least my own guard hadn't betrayed me on purpose.

No one from the school administration came to give me a final farewell. Strange. Usually they made a big showing, but I guess at 3 AM it didn't matter. And I suspected no one wanted me that close to their thoughts right now, even if they didn't know the whole truth.

"*Drake?*"

'I'm here,' he said in a gentle voice.

"*I'm scared. What if they don't put us in the same hospital? What if we can't escape?*"

Even my mental voice wavered from unshed tears. We risked so much, banking all our hopes on an untested possibility. We could be wrong. So very wrong.

'I'm scared too, but we have to believe this will work out. What choice do we have?'

He was right. Even if this plan—hell, it wasn't even a plan, really, more like a pipe dream inspired by desperation—but even if we knew for a fact that it wouldn't work, what else could I do? We had no way to escape, nowhere to go, no one to call. This had to work.

Gar loaded my luggage into the limo, ushered me into the back seat, and hopped into the driver's seat. As usual, we headed to our private airstrip.

'Sam, he doesn't know what's going to happen to you. You have to tell him. He might be able to help you escape.'

"*But I need to find you first. I can't go now.*"

'You must take this opportunity. There might not be another one. Once you and the baby are safe, I'll find a way to get to you. Please, Sam, you have to try.'

"*He has a little girl. What if we get caught? It could ruin his career.*"

'*Let him decide what he's willing to do. Don't make him complicit in your fate without giving him a choice.*'

My hands shook in fear. He had a point. If Gar really was trying to keep me safe, shouldn't he know the truth, even if that knowledge placed a heavy burden on his soul? More than my life was at stake.

We had maybe ten minutes before we'd reach the plane. Once there, I'd lose my chance.

"Gar, I need to tell you something."

CHAPTER 17 – SAM

The car slowed to a stop by the side of the road. Gar hadn't said a word while I told him everything—about Mr. K, Higgins's lies, the evil doctor... my pregnancy.

As hard as it had been to talk to Luke, Lucy and Drake about the baby, telling Gar had been one hundred times harder. He could report me, turn me in, betray me. But then, would I really be any worse off?

No.

So I waited for him to speak.

"Gar?"

He turned to face me, his hazel eyes and hard face revealing nothing. "What do you want to do?"

What did that mean? "Do you believe me? Did you already know?"

I knew the answer, but I wanted him to tell me he had nothing to do with this mess.

"I've known for a few months that something wasn't right. I've been keeping an eye on you ever since we returned from your last assignment. When I found out about the art studio fire, I looked into it, and some things didn't make sense, but it doesn't pay to get too curious about the people we work for. I have a family to consider, but I also knew I had to keep you safe. I thought getting you off campus and to New York would be enough."

"So now you know. I'm not going to New York." Saying it out loud made it feel much too real. I wanted to swallow the words back into my throat and pretend it wasn't true, that none of this was really happening, but feigned ignorance would not save me.

My mind flashed to an old Calvin and Hobbes cartoon I'd seen years ago. They were sliding down a mountain on a sled as Calvin spouted that the value of ignorance is bliss. Once we know something, he argued, we are forced to consider personal change in order to fix the problems that we see. If we persist in ignorance, we can stay cocooned in our beliefs — we can remain happy. At the end, when they fly off a cliff and crash, Hobbes remarks that he can't handle this much bliss.

In my heart I knew that to stay blind would not lead to any happy endings, and my fall off the proverbial cliff would not result in a witty barb, but rather an end to everything that mattered to me. No matter how unpleasant the truth, I had to face it and change my life to fix the problems.

Gar studied me as if searching for words he rarely used. I could imagine him opening up the container in his mind that held language, and dusting off all those unnecessary sentences and paragraphs.

Before he could respond, his walkie-talkie blared to life. "Do you need assistance? Our monitors indicate you've stopped."

I sucked in a breath. "Who's that?"

Gar looked around as if we were being watched. "Like you, the car has a tracker, and so do I. They monitor when we leave, to make sure we go straight to the airfield without incident."

Nausea bubbled up in my stomach, and I willed myself to keep my party food down. Between the utter exhaustion of leaving in the middle of the night, the emotional drain of keeping up a façade at the party, and saying goodbye to my friends—and now this—I was surprised I could sit up on my own. I didn't realize they embedded trackers in the guards as well. Did the teachers and all the staff have them?

That could help explain why Mr. K hated it there. He wasn't the type who would like being tracked like a stray dog.

So even just pulling over for thirty seconds triggered a response. We had to respond with something that wouldn't raise their radar. "Tell them I'm sick, that you pulled over so I could throw up."

He nodded and spoke into the walkie-talkie. "The girl got sick. I pulled over so she could puke. Will be at airfield about ten minutes behind schedule."

"You're taking me there? Even knowing what they'll do?"

The car jerked into drive and Gar pulled back onto the street. "If we try to escape now, they'll find us before we reach the highway."

With trackers in our bodies and on the car, we didn't have any chance of making a run for it. There had to be another way. "What about removing our trackers? If they can't track us we could escape, right?"

The movie scene played in my mind. We cut ourselves open and remove the trackers. Gar finds the tracker on the car and disables it, then tosses his cell phone and we drive off like James Bond, never to be heard from again. Easy.

Gar eyed me in the rear view mirror and frowned as though he could read my mind. "I could remove our trackers, but with your pregnancy and without proper medical supplies, I don't want to risk that. They're buried pretty deep, and I could do more harm than good. Besides, there aren't many roads we can hide on. They'd find us."

I grunted in frustration, my James Bond fantasy destroyed by the onslaught of reality. "So what, we give up and you just hand me over as a human breeder?"

His face hardened. "No. We don't give up. We think of a better plan. We'll have a greater chance of escaping once we're in the air. The trackers don't work in flight. I can hijack the plane, which has a stock of medical supplies. I can then remove the trackers and get you somewhere safe. But we need more than just an escape plan. Do you have anyplace to go?"

"Yeah, kind of. But we need to find Drake first. They're keeping him prisoner at another facility — the one they're taking me to. He has friends on the outside who can help us."

Gar shook his head. "Nope. My job is to keep you safe. We can't risk going after your boyfriend right now, not with a half-assed plan and no back up. So, where do you want to go?"

Drake had been listening and chimed in. *'Go to Father Patrick's church. Tell him what's happened. He'll find a way to help.'*

"I don't want to leave you there. What if they hurt you when they find out I've escaped?"

'I'll be fine. I heal fast. Just get to the church. Please!'

This plan had too many holes in it, but it was all we had and we were running out of time. "Fine. Can you get me to Venice, California?"

Gar nodded.

I stared out into the dark. "What about you? Where will you go when this is over? Drake's friend can probably help you too."

He turned right and slowed down as much as possible without stopping. "We'll figure that out when and if this works. You have to know, Sam, that the odds are stacked against us. Now, I need to make a call before we get there."

He dialed his cell phone. "Honey, it's me. Yeah, remember what we talked about...? Now would be a good time to visit some family. Keep our girl safe.... I love you too. Bye."

Oh God, how could I let him risk his life and safety for me? He'd told me about his family, but now they seemed more real. "This is a bad idea. You have people depending on you. You need to do your job and forget about me."

'Sam, no!'

"He has a family, Drake. I can't let him do this!"

"My wife knew something like this might happen. She'd want me to help you if she knew everything. I can't walk away and leave you in their hands without at least trying to save you."

"Why?"

"Because... our daughter... she's special. Special like you and your friends. I'd hoped your school could help her, but now I need to make sure she's safe from them."

His mind pulled me in and memories of his daughter filled my vision.

***

"Daddy, Daddy, come quick!" A little girl with flaming red hair and emerald green eyes sat on the grass next to the lake.

Gar ran out, fear clutching his heart at the distress in his daughter's voice.

Dirty tears streaked her freckled face. In her hands a kitten shuddered and convulsed — dying.

"Daddy, she's broken. Fix her, Daddy, fix her."

Gar knelt down next to the little girl who owned his heart, and cupped her cherub face with his large hands. "I'm sorry, Baby, I don't know how to fix the kitten."

"I found her here, next to the lake. I think she was attacked by a bigger animal."

The snow-white ball of fur had streaks of blood on its belly, likely internal injuries. Gar knew she didn't have long.

"Serena, I'm sorry. You'll have to let her go."

He tried to pry the girl's hands off the kitten, but she used all of her 6-year-old fury to hold on without crushing the dying animal.

"Do you see that, Daddy? The world got sparkly and my hands feel hot."

Gar didn't see the sparkly world, but when he looked down at his daughter's hands, they glowed a bright white.

Shocked speechless, he watched as the light surrounded the kitten.

He didn't notice how pale Serena had become until the kitten sat up and licked her face.

"Daddy, I'm tired now."

He picked up his daughter and carried her home, with the kitten trailing behind.

***

Gar's voice jolted me out of the memory. "That cat hasn't left her side since. This was four years ago."

My voice came out in a whisper. "She's a healer. A powerful one."

"Yes. We've done our best to keep her gifts secret. After healing the cat, she couldn't get out of bed for a week. We'd hoped—"

"—that Rent-A-Kid would keep her safe."

If they ever found out about her powers, the rich and powerful would pay anything to live longer, to be healed from disease, and she'd be drained until nothing remained but a shell of that girl.

It made sense now, why Gar had become my guardian angel.

"Thank you."

"Don't thank me yet. We still have a lot of work ahead of us."

***

The seconds dripped into my veins like acid. Dread filled me each time I thought about our plan.

We were about to hijack a plane? That was insane. I mean, sure, Gar would be the one doing all the heavy hijacking, but I would be part of it.

He ignored my attempts at small talk, so I finally shut my mouth and prayed to whoever might be listening that we'd make it out alive.

When we neared the airstrip, the runway lights and buildings turned night into day and blinded me. It shone bright with one tall radar tower, an office for the air traffic controllers who doubled as guards — or maybe guards who doubled as air traffic controllers — and a hanger that fit two state-of-the-art jets.

We drove through a chain link fence topped with razor wire, and pulled up to the jet that had been prepped for my journey.

I did my best to put on a game face. If I just pretended as though this were another assignment, I might get through it.

The pilot stood by the plane with a clipboard in hand, presumably doing a last-minute check of everything, and the stewardess smoked a cigarette outside the hanger.

Gar pushed thoughts into my mind. *'There are two guards stationed at the entrance of the jet, two in the office, the pilot and the stewardess. I'm the only guard that will be on the plane once it takes off, so I can disable the stewardess and pilot and take over the plane.'*

As he opened my door and grabbed my luggage, I jerked my head an imperceptible amount to let him know I'd heard him.

A chill swept through me and I shivered, pulling my jacket more tightly around me. My flimsy party dress did nothing to protect me from the cold night air.

Gar greeted the pilot and handed off my luggage to the guards manning the entrance. The short, stout bald one took my luggage up the stairs and into the plane, then returned and stood next to his taller, lankier partner. They both wore all black and had guns holstered at their sides.

Once the luggage had been handled, Gar motioned for me to enter first, so I did.

So far so good.

Then Gar tried to follow me in, but the stout guard stepped in front of him. "Change of orders, we will accompany the girl this time. You're needed back at the school."

I froze at the top of the stairs, just before the door. Gar looked up at me, but I couldn't read his face, so I slipped into his mind.

'Must do something.... Need new plan.'

If he couldn't travel with me, we had no plan. But Gar didn't back down. "I've been given my orders. I'm to accompany her to her destination. Step aside."

Neither guard budged. "We've got it from here. Return to school and await further orders. You've been reassigned."

Gar smiled, perhaps the first smile I'd seen on him. It sat awkwardly on his face, like an ill-fitting mask. "I'm sure we can figure this out, gentlemen. Let me just check in and clear everything with the boss."

The guards both relaxed their postures and nodded. A quick read of their minds proved Gar's response fit with protocol. They had no reason to believe he would go against orders.

Gar's body tensed as he spoke in hushed tones on the phone. He nodded his head a few times, and I could tell he tried to stay casual in his stance, but his balled fists betrayed his anger.

The conversation ended, and every nerve ending in my body flared to life. Sweat trickled down my neck onto the collar of my jacket, and the moment stretched into eternity as I waited to see what, if anything, Gar would do next.

As much as I wanted to peek into his mind, I needed to stay focused and alert. Should I try to run, stay on the plane, scream, cry, pretend to pass out? A dozen thoughts flittered through my mind, a dozen ways to distract, to get attention off of Gar—but that might make his job harder.

With hyper-awareness, I focused on Gar's every muscle twitch and movement.

His left fist unclenched, and something slipped into his hand. A syringe. He was going to attack.

Oh God! My heart thudded in my chest so hard I was sure the guards could hear it.

Gar chuckled and used his right hand to pocket his phone. "Guess you boys were right. Sorry about the trouble. Do you mind if I use the jet bathroom before I go? It's so much nicer than the one in the office."

The tall guard shook his head. "Sorry, man. Orders are orders. No one else is allowed on the plane."

Gar shrugged. "I understand. Oh hey, you've got something on your collar there."

Before either guard knew what was happening, he leaned into the tall guard on the left and plunged the needle into his neck. In the same breath he pulled the other guard's gun from his holster.

The tall guard staggered to the side with his hands clutching the syringe. "What'd you... do... ack...." He tried to lunge at Gar, but fell to the side on the tarmac and passed out.

Gar's hand didn't shake at all as he pointed the gun at the other guard. "Your partner will be fine, eventually, but you need to step aside and let me on the plane."

Lollie, the stewardess, screamed and ran behind the hanger to hide. The pilot, hidden on the other side of the plane, radioed for help, and I searched for other minds.

"Gar, the other guards are coming and they're armed. Hurry."

The guard being held at gunpoint lunged at Gar just as I spoke, but he'd lost the element of surprise. Gar stepped aside, tripped him, and then pistol-whipped his head. The man fell into a lump on the tarmac near his partner.

Gar pushed me into the plane and closed the door behind us. "Sam, we need to leave now. It might be a rocky ride."

My voice cracked when I tried to talk. "What's going to happen?"

"I'm getting you to California. Seatbelt up!"

He moved to the pilot's seat and flicked switches and buttons. The plane rolled onto the runway.

It took me a few seconds—which felt like minutes—to strap myself into a seat. My stomach flip-flopped and my pulse raced.

I linked to the minds of those outside the plane and cringed at the chaotic thoughts flying around. I traced each thought to its core until their plans became clear. Fear paralyzed me. "Gar, the guards from the office, they're coming after us."

"Drake, you there? I'm scared."

'I'm here. Stay calm. Damn, I wish I could do something. I hate feeling so helpless.'

I wanted to stay lost in his voice forever, but the plane's movement pulled me back to reality.

Sirens blared outside. Gar's radio crackled to life, but he turned it off before anyone could talk.

Neither of us said anything. I didn't want to distract Gar from the task of flying the plane. Once in flight, we'd be safe. Presumably, he knew where and how to land in California so no one would be there waiting to capture us. I could get help. We'd be safe.

The plane accelerated and so did my heart's beat. *Thump-thump. Thump-thump. Thump-thump.*

I resisted the urge to throw up, but I did grab the barf bag just in case.

I needed to know what was happening, so I slipped into Gar's mind.

'Oh shit, they have RPGs.... We're screwed... have to hurry... can't let them get her....'

If Gar was scared, I was terrified. "What's an RPG?"

"Rocket-propelled grenade. Looks like a little rocket, like a long tube, and is shot from over the shoulder. You've seen them in movies."

Right, yes, I had. Those movies where everything gets blown to hell.

"Can they take down a plane?"

"Yes."

How can he sound so calm? Maybe he had a plan, a way out that I couldn't see.

A large boom broke through the silence of our thoughts and our plane spun and jerked.

I cried out as the seatbelt dug into my stomach. "Gar, what happened?"

"We've been hit, but I think I can still fly it. Hold on."

We were going to fly a plane that had been hit? What? Didn't planes need all their parts to fly properly?

He straightened the plane and tried to get it back on course.

My breathing hitched and suddenly oxygen was in short supply, or maybe that was just me and my fear.

Another explosion tore through the air. Through the window I saw the right wing tear off. Pretty sure we needed both wings to fly.

Gar tried to taxi the plane away from the people chasing us, but it couldn't outrun a rocket. A final explosion ripped through the engine, tearing open the fuselage and tipping my world on its side.

Darkness overtook me and I faded into a world where Drake and I ran through flowers, only the flowers turned on us and spat poison at us. Something hit me and my vision spun, dizzy....

"Sam! Sam!"

My eyes cracked open. Gar held my head as he tried to unbuckle me from the seat.

"Sam, are you okay?"

Everything hurt, but I was alive. So, there was that. "What happened?"

He pulled me from my chair and propped me up against another seat that had turned on its side. "They hit us with an RPG and the plane tipped. We can't fly it. I'm sorry."

Something crashed into the plane door. Gar stood in front of me, gun ready.

He couldn't face off against them; he'd die. "Gar, you have to go. Please. Get out while you can."

"It's too late, Sam. I'll try to keep them away as long as I can. Can you walk? Crawl? Anything? Try to get away if you can."

Where would I go? How would I get out? I didn't voice my hopelessness, because really, what was the point? What more could he do?

The two guards from the office dropped through the hatch they'd opened—definitely guards who doubled as air traffic control, judging by the soldier-like way they carried themselves. The guards trained their guns on Gar.

The younger guard on the right spoke first. "Give us the girl, now!"

Gar didn't budge or speak.

I slipped into their minds, then whispered so only Gar could hear. "The one on the left plans to dive and shoot while the one on the right tackles you."

Gar shot the shoulder of the guard on the right and pushed me behind a seat. I'd never been in a shoot-out, especially not one in a steel tube with sharp, metal plane debris everywhere. This couldn't be healthy for the baby.

The ringing in my ears made the gunshots sound like they came from deep space, or one hundred leagues under the sea.

In that frenetic moment, I couldn't read anyone, couldn't help and couldn't escape.

All I could do was watch as a bullet pierced through the leather seat and into Gar's chest.

Tears choked my throat. I threw myself on him. "Gar. No. Please. Don't die. Gar."

The guards tried to pull me off of him but I held on. His eyes flickered open once more.... "Be safe, Sam. I'm sorry." ...and death stole him forever.

Memories flooded my mind like a tidal wave of displaced water trying to find purchase on the slippery shore of impermanence.

The first time he kissed his wife.

The first time he held his baby.

Friday night family nights with pizza and movies.

Normal scenes that didn't match up with the man I knew only as a guard.

But he wasn't just a guard; he was a husband, a father, a son. He was a man with a whole life slipping away.

Somewhere in the world, a wife lost her husband and a little girl lost her daddy, all because of me.

A sharp prick cut through my neck, and hot fire coursed through my veins, then all went black.

CHAPTER 18 – SAM

I fought against the consciousness that threatened to bring me back to a reality I had no desire to live in, but my body refused to stay in the darkness. Once again, I woke up in a hospital bed—a trend I needed to change—but this time I was strapped down to it. I flexed my legs and arms, pulling on the restraints, *but whatever drugs they'd given me* made me weak as a kitten. No matter. Even my full strength wouldn't have enabled me to break free.

My heart raced as panic gripped me. Gar's face had haunted my dreams, and even awake I couldn't tear out the memory of his death. His blood no longer coated my hands, but that did nothing to ease my conscience. I now understood how Lady Macbeth felt, the compulsion to wash and wash and wash away the guilt of a stained soul.

Of course, that kind of stain never washed clean.

A tear leaked out of the corner of my eye. If I couldn't stay lost in my own dreams, I had to stay focused.

The sterile room offered no unique markings or identifying traits, just a sink, chair, bed, stool, and empty tray. Standard medical supplies lined the walls. Nothing helpful.

I instinctively reached for Drake.

And I reached too hard. *'Sam!'* His voice filled my head, crushing my mind with the volume.

"*Ouch! Shhhh... don't shout. My head is already pounding.*"

'I'm not shouting.'

I tried dialing down my link to him, imagining it like a volume control; now that the speakers lay closer, I didn't need it so high.

'Are you okay?' His voice stopped splitting my skull.

"*Yes. No. I don't know. Drake... Gar is dead. It's my fault!*"

'No. It's their fault, Sam, never yours. Where are you?'

I projected my room to him, and he did the same. Our rooms were identical, but that didn't mean much.

A nurse came in, and—

'That's her, my nurse!' Drake said. *'We must be in the same place.'*

At least we had that. Would we try another escape?

"Oh, you're awake!" She looked startled.

"*How long have I been unconscious?*" I asked Drake.

'Since yesterday.'

Twenty-four hours of my life, stolen. What had they done with Gar? What would they tell his family? He'd died trying to save me, and still I ended up in the hands of the enemy, pumped full of drugs.

What would all these drugs do to the baby? I forced myself not to cover my stomach in reflex.

Best to act ignorant for now, see what I can find out. "What happened?" I asked the nurse.

If her nervousness was any indication, she wouldn't tell me the truth, at least not out loud. "*Oh, I think it's best if I get Dr. Pana. He can explain everything.*" At five feet, with dark blond pigtails and freckles under her green eyes, she looked barely old enough to drink legally. Even I looked tall and grown up compared to her. Did adults even wear pigtails? Where did they get this kid?

'*I hope I don't get in trouble... she shouldn't have woken up... I hate this job... but the money... need the money... hope Mom and Nick are okay... can't afford to get in trouble again... hate keeping these kids here like animals... not right but what can I do... if only I'd never met these creeps... and getting her pregnant... so awful... wonder what the baby will be like... it's growing too fast... but the dad is totally hot... oh God... I need to stop thinking around her... but no... the drugs should keep her out of my head....*'

Maybe she would be an ally.

'*Can't stand being around these freaks... feel bad for them but they creep me out... no one should be able to do what they can do... not natural... not the way God made us... abominations... no... I'm doing the right thing... taking care of my family....*'

Or maybe not.

She left the room without looking back at me, and I left her mind alone when she started thinking of church and her weekend plans. Interesting that their attempts to control my powers had failed. But definitely advantageous to me.

At least we finally had a few things going for us. They didn't know I could still read minds, and Drake and I were together. Sort of. Now we just needed a way of getting the hell out of here. If not for myself, then for Drake and our baby—and so that Gar's sacrifice wasn't for nothing.

"We need a plan, Drake. We can't stay here."

'Agreed. If we can figure out a way to get these drugs out of my system, we'll have a better chance of escaping.'

With renewed hope, my impatience grew. How long would they leave me lying here in this uncomfortable position? My muscles ached and my head still hurt. My arms had some range of motion, but not much.

The door opened again, and Dr. Pana entered. His energy rushed into me and I fought the false calm it tried to induce. I would not be seduced by this man's powers.

"Hello, Sam, nice to see you again. You're a strong girl. We didn't expect you to wake up so soon."

His syrupy sweet voice, the kind of voice that plotted unimaginable tortures while telling you how lovely the day was, enraged me.

"So I gathered." I tried to keep the sarcasm out of my voice. Best to stay on neutral ground for now. "What happened?"

He chuckled as if we were old pals. Yeah right. "Oh, I think you know what happened. Your guard made a grave, and ultimately fatal, mistake in trying to escape with you. Did you put him up to that or did he go renegade on his own?"

The moment of truth. How much should I reveal?

Drake answered my question before I could find my own thoughts. *'You need to claim ignorance for as long as possible.'*

"And make Gar out to be the bad guy? After everything he did for me?"

'He's dead, Sam. Nothing you do now can hurt or help him. You need to protect yourself. He'd want that for you.'

Sometimes pragmatism and self-preservation left a bad taste in my mouth.

"I have no idea what happened, doctor. My guard went psycho, said he couldn't let me go free, that I would ruin everything."

Did I sound believable? I pushed into his mind and faced a wall, just like last time. When I pushed harder, a sensation of fingers wrapped around my mind and plucked threads of memory from me. Is this what others felt when I read them? I didn't think so.

"You can't read my mind, Sam, but I can read yours, and I know you're not telling me the truth. Maybe some time as our guest will loosen your tongue."

No... this isn't what others felt. This is what it felt like to have my own powers used against me. Shock stunned me, and my brain tumbled around trying to rearrange all I knew into something that made sense. When I put the final piece in place, I gasped.

Dr. Pana smiled, and the overwhelming sincerity of it scared me more than any blatant evil could. "I see you've finally completed the puzzle. Yes, I destroyed your precious art. You caused quite a ruckus with this organization, garnering attention we couldn't allow."

Grief and fear blasted through my body and shook me to my core. "And Mr. K?"

"He won't be bothering us again."

My heart shattered and my lungs stopped working. I coughed out a sob. The fingers around my mind tightened, and my grief burned into pure rage. He had destroyed my life, my dreams, and Mr. K. I would make him pay... for everything.

A stillness settled on my mind, and I stopped fighting his influence. Instead, I observed every detail of the experience, and then I noticed — he was clumsy, unskilled. He couldn't dig deeper, couldn't unearth my secrets. He may have had access to my powers, but he lacked my training and skill. I could use that against him, somehow.

Too much had happened, too many new revelations. I needed time alone to consider, to talk it through with Drake. And I needed access to my own body.

"Can you at least get these restraints off me? It's not like I'm a threat in my current state."

He pushed his body against my hospital bed, blocking any view I had of the door and trapping me in his scent—a cloying blend of too-sweet body odor and too-musky cologne. "That could be arranged. Just remember, Sam, you have no power here. I control you and everyone at this hospital. Don't resist me and don't fight me, are we clear?"

I smiled sweetly. "Crystal."

Like a snake, his skin slithered against mine as he undid the latches on my restraints. I rubbed my raw wrists and ankles, and stretched my sore, cramped body.

"Nurse Susie will be in shortly to show you to your room and explain the rules. Feel free to make yourself at home. We want you to enjoy your stay here, however long it might be." He turned and left.

I tested the limits of my battered body. When I stood, all the blood rushed from my head, leaving my feet feeling heavy and awkward, and my head pounding.

I gripped the railing of my hospital bed and pulled aside my gown to examine myself. Red and purple bruises had created a new map on my pale skin. My stomach curved out in a barely noticeable bump. I wrapped my gown around me before anyone else could see—just in time to avoid the prying eyes of Nurse Susie as she pushed open the door.

The shift of attention offset my balance, and I reached for the nurse's arm to steady myself. She started to shy away, but apparently remembering her job, put her hand on my waist to steady me. She helped me sit in the wheelchair and hold onto my IV pole, and we made our way down the hall.

Bare, boring beige walls led to my new room, which had a twin bed with a blue comforter that looked clean enough. A modest closet, a private—but basic—bathroom, dresser, desk, and a small nightstand by the bed made it seem less like a prison. Any apartment I could have found in the Big Apple would probably have been smaller. The remote next to my bed controlled a television hooked to the wall, beyond my reach. A small barred window overlooking the woods reminded me that I was still in prison. Once again, I wished for Luke's superpower of walking through walls.

"Your personal items have already been put away. I'll bring your meals at 7:30 AM, 12:30 PM and 5:30 PM. If you need anything else, just ring that bell by your bed, and someone will respond immediately." She said this as if to suggest that ringing the bell would be frowned on.

"Am I allowed to go outside, walk around or work out anywhere?"

She eyed me and placed her hands on her hips. "You'll get one hour of outdoor time every day after lunch. There's a gated courtyard where you can take a walk."

"Wow, this is just like I always imagined prison would be."

"I suggest you learn to appreciate what you have here. Not all are so lucky."

I thought of Drake, strapped down and drugged. When was the last time he got to exercise or move around? Better off than him, but lucky? Not so much.

The nurse left me alone in my room, with only the monotony of my new life to occupy my mind.

Thank God I still had my connection to Drake, but first I needed to get cleaned up. They'd stripped me of my bloody, torn dress, but I still smelled of airplane debris and death.

I pulled my IV across the room to my bathroom and used up what little strength remained to wash myself. Dirty water swirled into the drain, and I kept rinsing and washing until that water ran clear. If only I could cleanse my insides so easily.

Sapped to near exhaustion, I searched the closet for clothes—something familiar and comfortable—and found some sweatpants and a t-shirt. I took the IV bag down and pulled it through the sleeve in my shirt, allowing me to dress. I was tempted to tear the damn thing out, but my loving nurse probably wouldn't like that very much.

Once tucked into bed, and before sleep could overtake me, I reached out to Drake. "I think I have a plan."

CHAPTER 19 – SAM

I tried to infuse my mental voice with more authority and confidence than I actually possessed. *"We need to get your powers back. So I'm thinking I need to find a way to switch the medicine they have you on, so we can get the drugs out of your system. When your strength returns and you can manipulate people with your mind again, we can work together to get out of here."*

'That was my thought, too. Next time the nurse comes to replace the fluid, I'll look at the bag more closely and tell you what it's called. You can poke around in her mind to see where they keep it.'

"Sounds good. I'll just have to figure out how to get out of here to make the switch. I'm hoping they won't keep a pregnant girl locked up all the time. I need to walk around and stuff, to keep the baby healthy. Don't I?"

'I guess so. One of my foster moms had some complications while pregnant. She was forced into bed rest *for months. That's when I had to go to another home. It was too much for them. So I don't know.'*

No way did I want bed rest for months! "Great, thanks for the pep talk."

'Hey, just trying to be helpful. We might want to have a Plan B in place.'

"We're going to have to be careful. Dr. Pana can use my powers against me. He was also able to use Kyle's fire powers. I'm guessing Dr. Pana can tap into any paranormal's powers and use them. How can we possibly fight against that?"

'He's got to have some weaknesses, some way to gain the upper hand.'

"He's unskilled. It's like he's a kid playing with toys he doesn't understand. I don't know if that makes him easier to beat or more dangerous, like a kid with a loaded gun. If only I had your ability to control minds!"

'That would be awesome. Wait, I wonder... have you ever tried to use another person's power?'

'No, why would I?' The idea intrigued me, but I had no reason to believe it was even possible.

'Maybe you couldn't do it with most powers, but what about other mental powers? Your mind-reading is similar to what I can do. You gather information from their minds, and I manipulate information. Either way, we're accessing a person's thoughts. I bet you could do it if you tried. Maybe that's why we have this mental connection, because our powers are so much alike. And maybe... maybe that's why they paired us up, because they want kids with our combined power.'

That made sense, although the thought of them genetically planning our babies, with some nefarious, long-term plot, made me ill. No time to think of that now. Could I learn to control minds like Drake? I'd never tried it, but... how to start?

'Next time the nurse comes in make sure you're linked to me, and see if you can get her to do one small thing mentally.'

"Okay, but how?"

'Well, how do you read minds?'

I'd never really thought about it before. I'd always known how to do it. The hard part had been learning to control it. *"I form a link with them, like a colored chord that goes from my mind to theirs — kind of like plugging in a telephone. Once it's connected, the information flows through it. If I have to, I can go into their mind and extract more thoughts, not just the ones they're having in the moment, but previous thoughts. That's a lot harder, because it's not a neat filing system where I can just look up what I want. It's a mix of images, sounds and smells, all layered on itself. That's where the good doctor fails. From what I could tell, he can glean immediate and pressing thoughts from someone when tapped into my power, but he can't dig deeper."*

'It's not that different then.' He sounded more excited than he had before. Maybe we did indeed have a chance at succeeding. *'When you're in their mind to read it, instead of just receiving the flow, send information back. Implant it there like it's their own thought. We did something very similar when Luke and Lucy were under the influence of those drugs. Only, instead of pushing against a fog, you'll be pushing a specific thought or command, but the energy and focus are the same.'*

I remembered that feeling while in Luke and Lucy's mind, but the thought of my best friends filled me with a profound loneliness. I would probably never see them again, which seemed — unfathomable. Inconceivable.

'Sam, stay focused. We'll get out of here and then we'll help them. I promise.'

I had to believe him. So I would bide my time and wait for a chance to practice mind control.

***

My opportunity came that night when the nurse brought me dinner.

The sound of the door opening woke me from a nap I didn't realize I had taken. She placed a tray of food on the table next to my bed. I eyed the funky looking meatloaf and Jell-O mold suspiciously, but knew I'd have to eat it if I wanted to keep up my strength. Besides, if they wanted to feed me drugs, they had a straight line to my veins. They wouldn't have to rely on my food.

Before the nurse could leave, I decided to practice the mind control thing. Who knew when I would get another chance?

"*Drake, are you ready?*"

'*Yes.*'

First I reached into her mind.

'*She thinks she's so much better than everyone because she has powers... just a freak... can't believe I felt sorry for her... can't believe they want to breed more like her... disgusting....*'

I focused my will and planted a thought.

'*You need to wash your hands... you should do that right now....*'

For a moment, I thought I'd succeeded, that her will would bend to mine, and a heady rush of power filled me. But then her will rose up and pushed me out with a violent force. My head exploded in pain and I cried out.

"What's the matter now?" She sounded bored, not angry or suspicious. How could she not notice? She must not have sensitivity to anything.

"Just a headache. Migraine."

"I can authorize a pain medication if you'd like."

As tempting as that was, I wanted to stay alert.

"No, I'll be okay Thanks."

She shrugged and left the room, and I slumped back into my bed, sad and defeated.

"*Drake, why didn't it work? It should have worked. I could feel it. I was so close.*"

'Don't give up, Sam. You just need more practice. It took me time to master this, and you're pushing it pretty fast. Try again once you recover. Next time, instead of talking to the person, reframe the thought as something they would think to themselves, like 'I need to wash my hands.''

That made sense. The compulsion needed to feel like it generated from within the person being controlled. I considered future commands and practiced them in my head while waiting for the next opportunity.

***

Instant success did seem unlikely, but that didn't make the failures sting less. Still, I didn't give up.

I used the same command over and over, and each time the headache lessened—marginally, but enough to offer hope.

By dinner the next night, everything clicked into place. As per usual, I compelled her to wash her hands, and then waited for the onslaught of the headache.

Only it never came.

Her will bent to mine, and it stayed bent.

"Excuse me, I need to use your bathroom to wash my hands." She walked to the bathroom, washed her hands, and then left my room with a slightly baffled look on her face. The lock clicked shut as she went back to wherever she spent her time when she wasn't sitting in judgment of me.

I'd done it! She couldn't have had that impulse to wash her hands in my bathroom at the exact moment I implanted the thought.

Drake's voice filled my mind. *'I knew you could do it. Now you just need to practice more, in small ways. They'll remember what they did, unless you also tell them to forget after they do it. You need to get good at that, because the things you'll want her to do later will raise huge red flags if she remembers.'*

"No kidding. I doubt she'll think it was normal to let me out of my room so I can swap your drugs. But, if I can control her mind, why not just have her swap the drugs, wouldn't that be easier?"

'Logistically it would be, but you would need to micromanage her mind and control each step of the process. If you slipped even once, you would fail. Getting someone to go against their own will, especially if it also violates their ethics, requires a tremendous amount of sustained power. It would be easier to lock her in a bathroom and compel her to forget, though there are obviously more risks to you if you have to leave the room and make the switch yourself. Speaking of that, I have the drug information you need.'

I grabbed a pen and paper and took notes, all the while wondering what would happen if she didn't forget as commanded, or if I got caught in the halls. We'd have to avoid Dr. Pana, or I'd be screwed.

***

It had been two and a half days, and I hadn't seen anyone but the nurse and Dr. Pana. That changed during my afternoon exercise hour.

My assigned guard, an average man in every conceivable way—nothing like Gar at all—was leading me back to my room. During the short walk, a doctor escorted a pregnant girl out to the lawn. The girl looked to be close to her delivery date. My guard grabbed my arm harshly, steering me down the hall, but in that brief moment I locked eyes with the girl. Tears formed in her eyes as we recognized each other.

Rebeka had been in a few of my classes, and I liked her. She was supposed to be in Paris, but of course she wasn't. Paris and New York were dreams spun from naive innocence, something we'd both lost.

Rebeka's doctor, a petite woman with long dark hair and brown eyes—eyes that struck a familiar chord in me, though I couldn't place her—nearly knocked me to the ground when she spoke directly to my mind.

'Please do not make a scene. Go back to the room quietly and pretend you do not see us. I'm your friend. I'm here to help, but they won't let me near you. Lock onto my mental signature and find me later. My name is Ana.'

"Who are you?"

'We'll talk more later. I must go.'

When I got back to my room, I told Drake about Rebeka and Ana.

'Be careful. I don't trust anyone who works here,' he said.

"I don't either. I'm just surprised to find another mind reader. Wonder why I couldn't sense her during my scans?"

'I don't know, maybe she has a way of blocking someone else. That would be cool if you could learn that.'

"Yeah, well, one thing at a time."

We hadn't made much progress with our get-out-of-jail plan, but my mind-controlling abilities had improved. It seemed I was a natural—a big plus for us. It was like a game, to see what I could do, how far I could push it.

Over the next several days, I kept to little things that no one would notice or suspect, except for erasing memories. It worked. This gave me hope, though I was still too nervous to do anything major, and I never tried it while Dr. Pana was around. I had no idea if it would work on him, and I had no desire to alert him to my new abilities. Whenever he came to my room, I kept my mind clear of anything incriminating.

I'd adapted too easily to controlling other people's minds. Sure, it was for the right reasons, but it felt wrong. Should I, or anyone, have the right to alter people's thoughts and control them in that way? Yet I'd spent my life spying on people's minds for

Rent-A-Kid, and I still used my powers as if mind reading was less invasive than mind control. In a way, it was, but I began to understand why Nurse Susie considered me an abomination. Whether reading minds or controlling minds, we still violated people's privacy and took something from them in the process. Still, we were born this way. We were used and locked up because of these gifts, so it seemed reasonably moral to use our para-powers to escape.

These moral arguments tumbled through me and became my shadow companions, taunting me each time I practiced my powers.

Drake had a similar schedule to mine, but we never met. They didn't let us near anyone else, but I could tell through my mental scans that there were at least three others in the building.

I learned about the video surveillance and the doors with special scanners, which only worked with certain staff ID cards. Dr. Pana, Nurse Susie, and one other presence further away whose thoughts were unusually fuzzy, revealed little. Was that Rebeka or Ana? Why couldn't I lock onto Ana's signature like she said? Where might the others be? Perhaps they had Rebeka on a drug that kept her mind hidden?

I worried about her being here too. I wanted to save us all, but we had to get out and find help before we could assist anyone else. Sort of like the oxygen masks in the airplanes—you have to save yourself first, or everyone dies. Something like that.

Again, pragmatism reared its ugly head.

I worked to cultivate patience and keep my body strong. When in the yard, I walked, did lunges, pushups, sit ups, and running in circles. My muscles burned in new and painful ways, and the heat sent bile rising to my throat regularly. At least they unhooked the IV during this time. It was a relief to be free, in a manner of speaking.

I kept an eye out for Ana or Rebeka, but hadn't seen either of them again.

I didn't think continuing the workouts would hurt the baby, though I only knew about pregnancy what I'd learned from television and biology class. I wasn't a badass or anything, not like Lucy. My mental gifts had demanded that I focus on my studies. I knew some basic moves, but I pretty much sucked at martial arts and hand-to-hand combat. Drake would have to handle that if necessary.

Rent-A-Kid required us to stay in top shape for health and longevity, yet, despite my best efforts, my body grew weaker every day, even as my powers grew stronger. It was as though the baby drained my body to feed my mind.

While outside one afternoon, all my senses kicked into hyper-focus. The chain link fence imprisoning me screeched in a high-pitched whine as the wind blew against it. My body flooded with sweat as the sun beat down. My belly ached, and even the skin on my abdomen burned as if stretched and torn.

The changes were happening so quickly!

My once flat stomach pushed out before my eyes. I half expected a monster to burst through my skin, like that scene in *Alien*. I doubled over in pain, fighting tears and trying to slow my breath.

'Sam, what's wrong?' Drake could feel my distress.

I sensed his fear and worry. Staying conscious required all my focus, too much for me to talk, even mentally. Especially mentally. I summoned the guard, who ran to my side.

"I feel sick. Need to lie down."

He steadied me with his right hand and led me back to my room.

I dressed in a baggy shirt so no one would notice my new bump. Not because of looks—though the idea of being huge the first time I met Drake in person didn't thrill me — but because I didn't want them to declare me pregnant. I needed to keep my freedom as long as possible.

We clearly needed to step up the plans. I couldn't keep my condition secret much longer.

I ran my hand over our baby, and the hard bump moved slightly. My hunger, which had gone missing recently, returned in full force. I used the much hated bell to summon the nurse.

Susie arrived with her arms crossed and a scowl on her face. "What?" *'I'm so sick of this job and these whiny kids... need to find someplace else to work... this sucks... how can she be so stupid to not know she's pregnant?'*

"It's nice to see you too. I got sick during my break outside and—"

"I told you not to exercise."

"Be that as it may, I think it was from hunger. I know dinner isn't for a few hours, but could I get an early snack?"

She glanced at my stomach and looked quickly away. I pretended to be looking somewhere else. My clothes hid the bump. I just needed to keep the staff away from my body.

"I'll bring you something."

"Thank you...."

She left before I finished talking.

Ten minutes later, I had my fill of green Jell-O — hardly real food — and almonds, with a little box of milk. I hated milk, but forced myself to drink it.

I rested after my mini-meal, my body at peace for the moment.

My eyes flew open. Our baby fluttered inside my belly like a butterfly, and a new consciousness swished through my mind. Our baby had linked to me.

"Can you feel this?" I asked Drake.

I tried to feel the sensation mentally, and our baby's mind connected with both of us. The link filled me with profound joy and love, such as I'd never known. I could sense her. I knew her.

Her. Our baby was a girl.

"*Drake?*"

'*I sense her too. I feel it. She's beautiful. Amazing.*'

We held this moment in a bubble of time, afraid of bursting it, of facing the realities of our situation.

"*What should we name her?*"

He laughed. '*I'm sure the name will come to us.*'

"*Drake, it's time. We can't wait any longer. Are you ready to move as soon as the drugs are out of your system?*"

'*Yes. But, Sam, be careful. I can't stand the thought of anything happening to you or our baby.*'

"*I will.*"

I hoped.

CHAPTER 20 – SAM

Our plan should have been simple. In theory.
Reality didn't agree.
Nurse Susie came into my room with dinner at the expected time.

"Is the doctor here tonight? Will he be checking on me?" I prayed for "no."

"He's gone for the night. He'll check on you tomorrow."

I didn't have long, but that removed a major complication at least.

I linked to her mind. *'So sick of my life... where else could I go... money helps... never get this kind of pay as nurse somewhere else... do people think I'm pretty?... she's really pretty... boys must love her... it's not fair... she gets it all... but I guess not since she's trapped here and doesn't even know it... stupid girl... I thought these paranormals were supposed to be smart?... six hours left on my shift and already I'm exhausted... what do I need to do?... that boy needs a change in IV... I'll do that after this....'*

Perfect!

I implanted a thread into her thoughts—a command, really. *"I'm not feeling good. I'll leave my keys and badge on the dresser. I won't remember leaving them. I feel so sick, and I'll be stuck in my bathroom for ten minutes. I won't remember being sick. I'll keep the door closed and not respond to anything for ten minutes."*

I put the full force of my will behind this instruction.

"I'm not feeling well." Nurse Susie dropped her keys and badge on my dresser and darted to the bathroom, locking the door behind her. She'd left my bedroom door unlocked.

I pulled my IV out, grabbed her keys and badge, and slipped into the hall, heart pounding so loud I thought for sure everyone could hear it. Her thoughts, and my brief moments outside, revealed that there weren't many people in this building.

I pulled images from Susie's memory to find the room with the medical supplies.

Cameras monitored the halls and rooms. I had no idea if my powers would work like this, but I scanned everyone I could find within a fifty-foot radius.

Susie... sick in my bathroom. Drake... anxious for me to finish. Dr. Pana... reviewing paperwork—oh crap. She said he was gone for the night. What was I going to do?

I had to move forward. We were out of time and Drake needed me.

Focus! I scanned more minds, found the one I needed—the security guard who controlled the cameras—and linked with him.

'Bored... need a cigarette break... don't really need to be here... nothing ever happens... wonder if I should call that babe from the bar last night... she was hot... should wait... make her wonder....'

I planted some commands. *"I'm bored. I need a break. I'm going to go smoke a cigarette. At least ten minutes. I'll take my time. Nothing ever happens here. Better switch off the recorder before I leave and forget I did it. Blame it on a power surge."*

When I knew he'd left, I squeezed through a crack in my door and made for the closet that held the IV bags. I stumbled, dizzy, perhaps from so much use of my powers, or maybe the pregnancy, or nerves. The concentration required to focus on so many minds made the simple act of walking difficult, but this was our last chance.

"I'm here. I'm switching the labels now."

'Be careful, Sam. Please.' His voice thickened with desperation.

I shook and jumped at every perceived noise, but at least I walked around freely. *Must follow the plan. Be proactive.* These assholes had Drake chained up like a dog. What would that do to someone like him? Someone so strong?

I used Susie's keys to open the closet, and found the IV bags. Drake's drugs, which looked just like the saline, were labeled with his name. I switched the labels with the saline bags and then switched the bags, disposing of his meds so no one would grab one by mistake. Now he should just get saline, and his system would be cleansed of whatever concoction they'd run through him.

I headed back toward my room, trying to avoid anyone else, and did a mental check on the doctor, Nurse Susie, and the guard. All were still in place, just as planned.

'Sam, you okay? Did it work?' Drake's voice quivered.

"Yeah, no problems. Just staying focused until I get back to my room."

I rounded the corner to my room, and —

Crap! He must have just left his office.

***

"What are you doing out of your room, Sam?" The doctor tried to stay in control, but the edge in his voice and his bright red face betrayed him.

Bile rose in my throat, but I swallowed and tried to cover my fear with concern. "Nurse Susie is sick in my bathroom. I don't know what's wrong with her, so I came looking for you."

Years of role-playing had made me a convincing liar, but that wouldn't help if he used my powers against me. I filled my mind with the reality of a sick nurse.

When his slimy mental fingers crawled over me, he heard what I wanted him to hear.

With the keys and badge hidden in my jeans pocket, I led him to my room. I linked with Susie on the way, amending my orders so she would remember being sick after all, but would not remember leaving her keys and badge. I would have to find a way of getting them back to her.

She still occupied the bathroom when we walked into my room.

I gave the doctor a knowing look. "Let me check on her first. She might not be decent." I headed for the bathroom before he could object, and mentally told her to unlock the door.

Once in the bathroom, I put her keys and badge in her pocket, and "told" her to forget that I did, and that she was feeling better and should explain to the doctor.

We walked out of the bathroom together. The doctor stood with his arms folded, a frown on his face.

"I'm sorry, doctor. I think it was something I ate for lunch. I'm feeling much better now."

And she looked better, though still a bit pale.

"You can never leave the patients unattended like this." He looked at me with renewed suspicion, and turned back to her. "It puts everyone at risk."

"Where is your IV?" he asked me.

I'd forgotten all about it. "I had to take it off to get help. I tried ringing the bell, but no one came, and I was worried."

I sat on my bed as Susie reattached the IV.

"Everything is fine, Doctor," she said. "I'm sorry she bothered you with this. It was just a bad food reaction."

I'd probably gotten her in trouble, but I had a hard time feeling too bad about it. To avoid suspicion, I linked to the guard, told him to get back to his station and get the cameras up.

Mind control had become second nature to me. So much for ethics. No wonder Susie hated me so much. I might hate me too, one day.

***

The doctor and Susie left the room. I sighed and fell back on the bed. Not *my* bed. Once upon a time, Rent-A-Kid had been home to me—dysfunctional as hell, but still home. Dreams of New York had gotten me through the rough patches. Now I had only myself, someone who'd let everyone take advantage of her for eighteen years. What good was I to my baby?

'You have me,' the comforting voice in my head whispered.

Yes, Drake and I were in this together. We hadn't met in person, yet I felt as if we'd been friends since childhood, just waiting to see each other again after a short time apart. When you're linked to someone in such an intimate way, it's impossible not to develop that strong bond. Or kill each other! Add to that a baby and... we couldn't turn back.

'Nurse Susie is here to change my IV.'

We both stopped breathing, waiting to see if she noticed the switch—the make-or-break moment in our plan. At least, the first such hurdle we'd have to clear.

How would we get out? Where were we? Where would we go? Who would help us? Who would believe us? Too many questions. No matter. I wasn't going to die here, unless it was while fighting for our freedom.

'She's done. She didn't seem to notice anything different.'

"Do you notice anything different?" Was it too early to hope?

'Not in my powers, but this doesn't burn me inside like the drugs did. It feels cooling and cleansing. My mouth doesn't feel stuffed with cotton balls anymore.'

I closed my eyes, took a deep breath, and held it for a few seconds before releasing it in a slow sigh.

"*So now we wait.*

"

CHAPTER 21 – SAM

I'd never expected to play hero, and didn't really want the role. Several other paranormals would have been better at this than me. Not for the first time, I wished for another path, a normal life in New York. My wishes were made on dead stars, it appeared.

I stretched my body and raised my arms to the sun during my daily exercise routine. My reinvigorated appetite had made my body stronger. Still, my pasty skin and flaccid muscles did not approve of me. I did my best with the time and body I had.

Three days had passed since we'd made the switch. Drake still didn't have his powers back, and I couldn't fathom another possible way to escape. We would both need access to our full powers. Already it seemed an impossible feat.

I finished stretching and went into a push-up/sit-up/strength-training routine, pushing myself not to give up. Superhuman body parts might not have been part of my special powers, but I would use what I did have to maximum effect.

"*Drake, how do you think they find us?*" I sweated through my T-shirt in the hot sun.

'*I don't know. I've been trying to figure that out myself. They didn't find me for a long time, which seems odd. Maybe because I moved so often.*'

"*You were a secret ninja!*" I joked. Not very funny. "*What if they have a seer, someone who finds us with a third eye kind of thing? How do we escape someone who can do that?*"

'*I don't know.*'

"*I've been thinking. We both use mental powers to manipulate the mind. What if we could figure out a way to join our powers, strengthen our ability to control those frequencies, and link with whoever tries to find us? Link with them and mislead them?*"

The idea had been building in my mind for a while.

'*That's a brilliant idea, Sam. And it just might work. We should try it here, see if we can link to people farther away. Maybe we can start with your friends. You couldn't link to them alone, but maybe together we could. That will give us a sense of our power and range.*'

"*I'm not going to start controlling my friends.*" I felt bad enough doing it to anyone. I was not about to start adding people I loved to this.

'*Of course not. We'll only practice that skill if they let us, and only with things they approve. Agreed? Whichever twin we practice on, the other can tell us if it worked.*'

Would this harm them? I didn't know. Let them make the choice on their own. We had to know what we could do.

"*Okay, but if they're uncomfortable with it, that's it. No pressure!*'

'*Should we try now?*'

My guard stood by the hospital door, not really watching me, but obviously there because of me. Impossibly high electric fences surrounded the area. What did he think I would do out here by myself? Sprout wings and fly away?

I sat on the bench by the empty basketball court... an ironic venue given they only allowed us out here alone.

I rested my elbows on my knees. To anyone observing, I would look as if I were cooling down from my work out.

"Ok, I'm ready."

It's not as though we had an instruction manual for this, so we both just linked and imagined our minds as one. The sensation frightened me. My mind and thoughts expanded to include his, and I felt his do the same. It wasn't like the one-way link I normally made, nor was it like the mind-talk link we had going.

We immersed ourselves in each other — mentally naked, vulnerable, scared. After a lifetime of hiding who I really was from almost everyone, to stand before anyone completely raw made me jittery. So be it. We had to save ourselves.

I waited for the judgment, the pulling away, the fear.

Instead, I found a kindred spirit. He too expected judgment and feared the loss of our intimacy when I saw his true self.

But I'd dreamed his memories for so long that the little boy he had been transposed over the man he had become — and I saw all of his true and complete self.

His anger and violence, the dark shadows that haunted his soul, made sense in the context of the life he'd been given. I embraced it all and offered him sanctuary inside my heart.

In return, I found my own solace in his.

How I wished we could stay in that moment, relishing the magic of each other, but we needed to see if we could connect to Luke and Lucy.

He followed my lead, since I knew what mental vibrations to look for. It wasn't so much like traveling over a geographic area as turning to the right channel on the television.

When the link switched on, it flared strong and sudden.

Lucy screamed in my head, and we almost dropped the link. Luke's thoughts drifted next to hers, which surprised me. I'd never linked with so many people at once—like a party in my head. I suddenly had an image of *Being John Malkovich*.

"*Shhh, calm down. It's me, Sam. Drake is here too. We're testing our combined powers.*"

'*Oh my God, Sam, I've been worried sick about you!*' *I could hear the tears in her voice.*

"*Are you okay?*"

'*We're fine,*' Luke said. '*It's been hard without you here, and all the staff is getting weird. We haven't managed to send pictures to Drake's friend. They're cracking down on security since you left. Even assignments have been cut back.*'

'*I wonder what's going on,*' Drake said.

"*Oh my God, you guys, Rebeka is here. And very pregnant. She looked miserable.*" I'd tried to link with her several times, but couldn't find her. I worried something terrible had happened.

Lucy sounded sad. '*That's awful. She was sweet. Her para-power should have been kindness instead of seeing through walls.*'

"*Yeah, it broke my heart to see her. Oh... and it gets better. I'm starting to show. We're going to have to escape soon, before they realize I know everything.*"

My head pounded as if a team of construction workers had moved in. How long could I maintain this link? My muscles spasmed, and sweat flowed from my head in small rivers.

We explained quickly. Much to my friends' credit, or insanity, they readily agreed to be guinea pigs for us.

We experimented, making Lucy jump up and down, Luke sit in the corner, and Lucy stand and sit over and over. We had to sync our thoughts and focus really hard to make it happen. We had a lot of misses at first, but we figured it out through trial and error, and our successes became more consistent.

"Thank you for letting us do this," I said. *"What does it feel like?"*

'It's like your body and mind split,' Lucy said, *'and somewhere inside, you know you're not in control, but then it doesn't matter. Those times you told me to forget, I have no memory of anything.'*

"You are the best friends. I miss you so much. We will escape, and we will find a way to get you guys out. I swear. I wish we were all together, in our apartment in New York, debating what to do on a Saturday afternoon. Not living this nightmare."

'Hang in there, Sam. We'll all make it through,' Luke said. *'And Drake, you'd better take care of her and that baby, or I will find you and make your life hell.'*

I missed Luke. I missed both of them so much it nearly crushed me.

Much to Drake's credit, he accepted my friend's threat in good humor, promising to do anything it took to keep us safe.

I hung on to the link longer than I should have, not wanting to say goodbye to my friends. When my nose started bleeding and my head hurt so bad I nearly passed out, I forced myself to break the link. Tears rolled down my cheeks and onto the hot gravel at my feet.

At times, when I thought about what we were up against, I feared our task would be impossible.

Then I felt my baby swimming in me, reminding me with a gentle mental tug that hopelessness was not an option.

Now we knew we could control willing subjects from a great distance. Our test had been successful, the knowledge gained useful. The headaches, not so much.

When my hour was up, I slogged back to my room, showered quickly, and slept for most of the afternoon.

***

I didn't make it two days before my only wardrobe choices came with elastic bands, as my belly swelled too much to suffer through buttons and zippers. Not as if I had to dress nice for anyone, stuck in a room alone all day. My "dates" with Drake didn't exactly require a dress code.

"What do we do when we get out of here?"

'What do you mean? Like how do we take down this whole organization?'

"That, yes. And us. I have no home, no life outside these walls. No one even knows I exist. I have no ID, no last name even. How will I survive out there?"

I didn't really expect an answer, but it helped to talk to about it all. The terror of failing burned like a wildfire in my chest. The fear of success sat like a brick in my stomach. I didn't want to become a ghost in the world. A nobody.

Who was I without proof of life? No birth records or identifications. No passports or parents. I didn't even exist outside of Rent-A-Kid, and neither would my baby. To get a job, make money, pay taxes—all these things required paperwork I didn't have. I'd seen enough of the world out on assignments to know there was only one place for people so far off the grid. They became the nameless, faceless masses on the streets.

'Sam, you won't be alone. I won't leave you on the streets to starve. You have me and I have friends. We'll find a way to survive.'

His comforting words played like a lullaby in my mind.

I tossed and turned with restless dreams that night. Nightmares, really — images blurred together, evoking a sense of fear and failure. I woke up in a sweat, tangled in my sheet, with my hair matted to my face and neck.

'Sam, can you hear me?'

"Yes. Is something wrong?" My clock said 2:30 AM. No wonder I felt like crap.

'I have my powers back. The drugs are out of my system!'

All sleepiness vanished. I sat up in bed, and we talked about our next step. We'd been planning and talking about this forever, it seemed. But still, this step was crucial. We had no idea of the repercussions if we failed.

We decided to get some rest and plan our escape for the next night. We needed all the advantages we could get. We'd have the night guard disable the cameras and open our doors. Then we'd meet up, "borrow" the guard's car, and escape.

Simple enough, right? Sure.

***

I woke up vomiting, with fire burning through my gut. My stomach had doubled in size, and the pain threatened to tear me apart.

Nurse Susie rushed me to another part of the hospital on a gurney. Dr. Pana met her halfway down the hall, as I moved in and out of consciousness. Drake worried somewhere deep in the back of my mind, but I couldn't respond.

Several scans later, and God knows what tests, they gave me something to ease the pain and relax the baby. She moved inside me, growing, trying to break free of the confines of my body. I tried to link to her, to tell her it wasn't time.

Maybe it was. How did I know? This was no normal pregnancy.

Oh, my God, what if they genetically altered her somehow? What have they done to us? These thoughts consumed me for the rest of the day, but I didn't have the strength to read minds, and Dr. Pana never left me alone long enough to try.

Still, I didn't need my powers to know that my baby was dying, and so was I.

Chapter 22 – SAM

We had little time left. I'd only been able to set Drake up with enough saline to last no more than a week. He'd already used four days' worth, leaving us three days to escape before the real drugs returned and he lost his powers again. We couldn't—

I noticed the smell first—a mix of alcohol and baby powder. Then the crying.

I lay in yet another sterile hospital room. Across the hall, where the crying originated, was a closed door marked Nursery. Not many babies, maybe two by the sound of it. A woman in a lab coat entered my room and pulled the curtain, blocking my view.

'Sam, keep your eyes closed and pretend to be asleep.'

It was Ana, the woman I'd met with Rebeka. I got a closer look at her before feigning sleep. Her large kind eyes, the color of chocolate, were genuine and warm—nothing like the doctor's. Her lilting accent—Spanish, I think—gave her voice a musical quality. Going against all logic and reason, I liked her instantly.

I hesitated a moment, then opened my mind to explore hers, hoping she was someone I could trust.

'I know you can hear me, Sam. And I can hear you. We share gifts, you and I, so listen to me. Do not try anything reckless right now. You and your baby are in danger. Do you understand?'

I almost had to pinch myself to return to the moment. *"Who are you? Why are you working at this horrible place?"*

I could feel that she didn't belong here. This life made her sick with anger and fear.

'There is more to the story than you can see right now, but I am a friend. I know you have no reason to trust me, but I'll try to help you and Drake. He's in danger. They can't control him for long, and once he's harvested, they'll kill him.'

My heart sank to my feet, waiting to be stampeded by the cruel world that enslaved me.

'Stay asleep. They're watching us. I know the medication they put you on to control your powers isn't working. They don't know this, which is the only reason they allow me around you. I'm the only doctor they have that can fix the mess they made with these pregnancies, so they have to let me treat you. Don't despair, child. I was once in your position, a student at what you call Rent-A-Kid.'

"If you were one of us, why are you helping them?"

Despite how much I liked this woman, my anger bubbled out. And why shouldn't it? We'd all had our lives ripped from us, torn apart by these greedy bastards who only wanted to use us for our powers.

'I know it doesn't make sense, but... please know that I have my reasons. Unlike you, I didn't have help. If I hadn't stayed on, they would have killed my children.'

Of course! That niggling sensation of familiarity—her eyes, her smile. Just like Lucy. The shape of her face—exactly like Luke's. Twins never happened at Rent-A-Kid. Except them. I probed her mind deeper than normal, delving into thoughts hidden well beneath the surface. Images flashed at me: babies born, her fear and love, her holding them and kissing them. Her losing them.

My own heart ached with her pain, as I watched her story unfold in my mind. *"Luke and Lucy are your children."*

Love filled her mental voice. *'Yes. I had them in this clinic almost eighteen years ago. I was your age at the time. They were allowed to stay with me while they nursed, but once they showed signs of powers, they were taken away and put in a special childcare center run by the organization.'*

Her children were my best friends. I loved them almost as much as she did. *"They were told they were abandoned at a hospital, left in the care of social services."*

'No. No! I would never have left them if I had a choice. I love them with all my heart. They keep me going.'

"I know. I saw. I can connect with them, and help you talk to them."

I'd seen into more than just her mind, I'd seen into her heart. I had to help this woman. She wouldn't hurt my friends or betray us. Besides, we were all dead if we didn't find someone to take our side.

'You can do that? You have that much power?'

"With Drake's help, yes. We've done it before. Would you like to meet your children?"

'Yes, more than anything. But not until you've rested and recovered. You nearly lost your baby, and would have died yourself. Your body has been through a significant strain. I can't let you push your powers while you're in this condition.'

"Is Rebeka okay?"

She worked on me, checking different parts of my body while we linked. When I asked about Rebeka, her hands fumbled. I felt a small tremor.

'I'm so sorry, but she and her baby died. I tried to save them, but the bastards wouldn't let me give her the treatment I'm giving you. They tried to manipulate the genetics of the child, controlling which para-power it would get. They don't just want to make more paranormal kids, they want to make kids with very specific gifts.'

Repulsed? Yes, but not surprised. I couldn't be surprised by anything they did anymore. They were monsters.

"*But why? What do they need to do this?*"

'I don't know, but these are long-term plans. Perhaps they've tracked which kids get the most money when rented out, and want more of those.'

Greed. Always at the heart of this organization.

"*Will you help us escape?*" Might as well lay it all on the table.

'If they catch any of us, we'll all be dead. And so will my children.'

"*Ana, Lucy will be eighteen soon. They'll breed her, and what do you think they'll do with her once they've used her up? Is that the life you want for her? For your grandchildren? Help us collect enough evidence to take this place down, and help us escape. Drake knows someone on the outside — a reporter.*"

'Do you promise you'll help my children?'

I wanted to help them, but how? I couldn't even help myself, and I had a baby to take care of. Would I be able to handle it all?

Ana saw my hesitation. *'I know you're scared. I'll help you and Drake. I know you'll do the right thing when you're free.'*

Her cool hand touched mine, a brief moment of human contact after so much isolation. I tried to stay still, asleep, but I wanted to jump up and hug her.

She said she'd be back as soon as possible, and left.

***

Then Dr. Pana came in. His evil stank up the room. I allowed myself to "wake up."

"What am I doing here? What happened?"

He trailed his finger over my exposed stomach, making my skin crawl. "Come now, Sam, you aren't stupid. You know more than you're letting on. You're pregnant, but you nearly lost the baby. Once you're stable, we'll move you to a new room. You're the only expectant mother here at the moment, so you'll have it to yourself. What you're doing is for the good of humanity. It's important. We wouldn't keep you here if it wasn't."

Propaganda bullshit!

"I want out of here. You have no right to do this to me!"

I kept my mental link with Ana, and added one to Drake. We explained our plan and how she could help.

'This is risky,' Ana said. *'I don't know if it will work, but I'll help. You're right: doing nothing will only ruin the lives of more children. It's time, after all these years, to act against them. I have files — names, dates, information I've been collecting for a long time. Like you, Sam, I was trained in spying and collecting sensitive information. A mind reader is rare in the paranormal world. It's why they let me live, and trained me to become a doctor. I was their greatest asset. But also, like you, their greatest threat.'*

'We need to act fast.' I knew Drake feared losing his powers again, but he sounded calm. *'I only have two more days of the saline replacements.'*

Out loud, I kept up a forced argumentative conversation with Dr. Pana — aware of his mental fingers latching onto my mind — while plotting mentally with Ana and Drake. I confused myself a few times, but we managed to create the beginnings of a plan.

"What will I do when we escape? What doctor will know what to do with me and my baby on the outside?"

'I don't know. You will need medical care.'

"Come with us," I begged her. "We need you. My baby needs you."

'The babies here need me too. They barely survived when the mothers died. And my children need me. If I leave, they'll hurt them. What if we can't rescue them in time?'

"But if we escape, won't they suspect that you helped us?"

'Probably, but I'll have to risk it.'

"Okay, I understand you can't come with us. I don't want anything happening to my friends. They're the only family I have too, you know. So we need to make you look innocent."

Drake jumped in. 'We'll have to hurt her, make it look like we, or I, attacked her to free you. It's the only way.'

"No!" I felt Ana and Drake flinch at my mental scream. "We can't hurt her. She's risking everything to help us!'

'No, he's right, Sam. It's the only way to make me look innocent and let you escape. If we don't convince them I wasn't involved, they'll kill my kids and me.'

As far as plans went, this sucked. I hated always being at the mercy of these jerk-offs. When did my life so completely fall apart?

"How do I keep my baby safe?"

'I'll give you enough supplies and drugs to care for you and the baby, and to slow down the growth rate. The medicine will work. Just remember to take it regularly.'

Our conversation ended, and Dr. Pana took me to my room and locked me in. Despair rifled through me, shooting darkness and fear into my heart. I let the pain gnaw at me, tear apart my hope, and when

I'd cried every last tear in me, I made a simple vow: no more of that—time to move forward.

I never got to see the babies, but in my mind, I heard their cries and the whispered lullabies Ana sang to them to lure them back to their dreams—the same lullabies she'd sung to Luke and Lucy when they were babies. Each lilting song broke a piece of my heart when I thought of how Rent-A-Kid had torn apart their family.

I lived in isolation again, without even the outdoors to look forward to, this time. Babies filled my dreams and consumed my waking moments. A part of me resented this newfound responsibility. I didn't want it. I was only eighteen, nowhere near ready to be a parent. I hadn't even met the father in person yet.

Ah, get over it. Stop the damn whining and just get on with it!

***

The next day we prepared for the great escape. It would happen late at night. Ana had arranged to be on the night shift. She seemed on the verge of tears, but she held it together. Drake was ready, sneaking in opportunities to strengthen his body. I was ready... mostly. My body felt stronger, but my heart raced uncontrollably from fear.

We had one more thing to do before setting out. We linked Luke and Lucy with Ana.

"Hey guys, sorry I haven't been back to talk to you. It's been a crazy couple of days, but... um... there's something I want to tell you about."

'Are you okay? What's happened?' Lucy didn't sound like herself. The stress of all this dampened her normally bright spirit, which made me even more determined to get out of here.

"You guys, your mom didn't abandon you. She was one of us. They bred her and took you away when you were

babies. She's here, linked to you now, and is helping us escape. Her name is Ana."

Silence. And shock. Their thoughts spun in a tornado that made it hard to keep up.

Ana spoke first. *'My children, I'm so sorry for what you've been through. I've done everything I can to keep you alive, to make sure you're treated well. I have loved you all this time.'*

'Mom? Are you really our mom?' Luke could not hold his tears.

'Yes, mijo, I am. And I never abandoned you. They stole you from me, just like they stole me from my parents.'

Luke's voice was strained. *'Who's our father?'*

'I don't know,' Ana said. *'I wish I could tell you, but I could never find the records. I'm sorry.'*

We kept the link open as long as we could. Ana and her children talked about everything, from favorite movies to their para-powers. Luke loved that Ana and I shared mind reading. It also accounted for Lucy's lie-detecting ability. Para-powers were shaped to some degree by genetics, though that didn't explain how the line of paranormals started in the first place.

The conversation went on for a long time. Hearing them all cry and talk at once hurt my head. I wanted to hug everyone.

The craving for physical contact surprised me. Most people didn't really think about it, normally. I would sit next to Luke and Lucy on the bed with our legs touching, or we would hug. Other friends would hug me or put an arm around me. Some level of physical contact was natural, something we didn't even think about.

But since being here, I'd gotten almost none. Ana would brush against me when she could, offering a hand of support. Susie tried not to touch me at all, and Dr. Pana never touched me except in creepy ways that made my skin crawl.

I'd never realized how much I needed to be touched, and to touch—to feel that contact with another person.

No one wanted to end the conversation, but we all forced our goodbyes. Still connected to Ana, I felt the tears flow down her cheek and drip over the edges of her smile.

'Thank you, both of you. Thank you so much. That meant the world to me.'

The group link had drained me. Would it affect our ability to escape? Maybe, but I didn't regret it. That one conversation healed a hole in my friends' hearts that had been raw far too long. I could see the light in Ana as well, brightness in an otherwise dark world.

This was real power. Not controlling other people, but helping to heal their hearts. For the first time in my life, my para-powers meant something more.

They made me proud.

CHAPTER 23 – SAM

Drake and I linked and commanded the guard to shut down the camera. Ana had slipped him a little something that would keep him in the bathroom for quite some time. She locked him in, and Drake and I instructed him not to leave, even if he started to feel better. Ana snatched the keys from the guard desk, and came to my room.

She pulled out a scalpel and walked toward me. The hairs on the back of my neck sprang to attention.

"I'm so sorry, Sam, but I have to do this."

This couldn't be. I didn't believe she would hurt me.

"You have a tracker in your arm. I have to remove it before we leave this room, or you won't get past the security gates."

My body visibly deflated. *Right, the tracker.* She reached for my right arm. I rolled up my sleeve, held it out and gritted my teeth.

The pain came without warning—sharp, biting. The blade sliced into me, dug through me, and pulled out. Warm liquid flowed down my skin. A metallic plop followed.

Ana wrapped my arm. "You're a very brave girl. Are you okay?"

I moved my arm to test it. The muscle ached, but I would live. "Yes, let's go get Drake."

She hid the tracker, a thin metal piece, in a drawer and grabbed a clean scalpel for Drake. I grabbed my backpack with my sketchpad and secret box tucked safely inside.

When we got to his door, I paused. This was the moment. Our first meeting. Ana had been kind enough to get me a pair of khaki pants that fit and a blue sweater that brought out the blue in my eyes. I'd pulled my hair back in a braid. No makeup, but I hadn't worn any in so long that I didn't really think too much of it. Still, the butterflies in my stomach turned into raging bees.

What if the chemistry we had in our minds didn't translate to our bodies? What if he looked at me and ran away?

Ana, reading my mind, tugged me to the door with a motherly smile. My heart clenched at the thought that Lucy and Luke should have basked in that smile over the last eighteen years. The injustice of it all renewed my motivation.

She opened the door and Drake stepped forward, and for that moment, the world stopped spinning and time stood still.

In my imagination, he hadn't been so tall. Tall and muscular. His blond-highlighted hair lay casually messy, and his crystal blue eyes held me in a long stare. He'd found a way to shave, and the chiseled strength of his jaw made my knees weak.

When he smiled, warmth filled my stomach.

"Sam."

That was it, just one word, but he made it sound like it held all the secrets of the universe. His voice was deeper, huskier, than it had been in my mind.

"Drake, it's really you."

He reached for my hand. "It's really me."

When his skin touched mine, lightning danced between us.

He pulled me close, breathing in the scent of me as our bodies touched. I nearly cried right there in his arms, just being held, feeling him. I never wanted to let go.

But I had to. We sighed and reluctantly pulled our bodies apart, though we clutched each other's hands as often as we could.

He held his arm out to Ana, having heard our thoughts, and she carved the tracker out. He didn't flinch, just held my gaze and smiled, as if she hadn't jabbed a sharp object into his bicep.

Ana wrapped his arm, and led us through a maze of hallways and rooms. They knew Drake could control minds, which would explain why she led us to the door. Her alibi.

She gave Drake her car keys and the keys from the guard. *'In the trunk, there's a blue backpack with a small memory stick in the inside pocket. It also has money, clothes, and supplies for you both—medical supplies for you, Sam, a laptop computer, and a cell phone that's not traceable. You'll also need the guard keys to get out the back way, through the locked gates.'*

Even though I wanted out of this hell, I couldn't stomach the thought of what we had to do next. They mustn't suspect her of anything.

Damn pragmatism.

Drake looked miserable. "I'm so sorry, Ana. Thank you so much."

Ana sat on the floor against the wall so she wouldn't fall, then smiled. "Just do it, *mijo*. It's okay. I'm tougher than I look. Just make it believable."

He released the super strength his muscles carried before punching her in the side of the head.

I cried out as she slumped to the floor, feeling his fist as if I'd suffered the blow.

CHAPTER 24 – DRAKE

Drake cradled Ana's head so she wouldn't fall to the floor, and positioned her in the most comfortable way possible before looking at Sam. He waited for anger, but he saw only love in her eyes.

He reached out and ran his hand through her silky hair. "I'm sorry."

Her eyes spilled over with tears, but she didn't pull away from him. He sighed in relief when she gripped his hand with as much desperate need as burned in him.

"I hate this, Drake, but we had to. Now let's get out of here before we're caught."

An ache eased in him. He had a new guardian angel, a soul who accepted him, shadows and all.

Drake was guiding Sam toward the door when a voice from the stairs froze them in place. "What the hell are you doing down here? Stop right there."

The security guard aimed his gun at them. *How did he get out?*

As soon as he'd thought the question, the answer arrived. Dr. Pana followed behind the guard with an evil grin spread across his face. "You two are not going anywhere." His calm, quiet voice was more terrorizing than if he'd been wild with rage.

A haze of compulsion settled into Drake's mind as Dr. Pana hijacked his powers and took control of him. He wanted to scream for Sam to run, but his mouth wouldn't open and he didn't know if she could hear him mentally anymore.

Sam's face turned hard. "Let go of him, Dr. Pana. Now!"

The clutches on Drake's mind released and he gasped in relief and pain.

Dr. Pana's face twisted in anger. "How?"

Sam still held center stage, so Drake used that moment to creep forward, ready to tackle the doctor.

Sam grinned. "You underestimated us."

'Drake, he can only use one power at a time. We have to keep him off balance.' Her voice floated through him like a cool breeze.

He took that opportunity and lunged, tackling the doctor to the ground.

Sam screamed. "The guard!"

From the corner of his eye, Drake saw the guard turn and point his gun at him. Time pushed against him like a viscous liquid, and he couldn't move fast enough to stop the inevitable.

The guard's trigger finger twitched.

Drake braced for the impact of a bullet.

But no gun fired. The guard's eyes glazed over and he threw the gun down the stairs.

Sam had intervened, but in letting go of the doctor's mind, she'd opened up the window he needed to seize Drake's mind again.

Under compulsion, Drake moved away from the doctor. Inside, his will fought the clumsy control the doctor exerted, but couldn't break it, and he recognized in that moment the energy of the man who had kidnapped him from his surfing contest.

Of course, Dr. Pana had been behind it all. Fury raged in Drake, seeking an outlet but finding none. His muscles flexed and pulsed, bulging tight against his jeans and shirt, coiled and ready but unable to strike.

The guard made for his gun, but Sam intercepted him and kicked the gun farther away, then latched onto Dr. Pana's mind again and released Drake from the control.

"You did this to me. You took everything from me." His fist landed in the doctor's gut and sent him flying down the hall, where he lay struggling to breathe.

Drake stalked forward, ready to finish off the doctor, but the guard pounced on Drake and wailed at him with ineffectual punches. Though no match for him in strength, the guard was small and fast, and Drake's counterstrikes landed on air.

A foreign energy infiltrated Drake's body as he fought the guard, and siphoned off his extra strength. The guard's punches bit deeper into his body and filled him with unexpected pain. Each blow disoriented him further, until his vision spun with flashes of light.

Drake raised a heavy arm and swung, but missed again.

The doctor groaned, healing himself with Drake's power, then pulled a gun from his pocket and aimed at Sam.

"No!" Drake's powers crashed back into him and renewed strength burned through his veins and flooded his muscles. His fist slammed into the guard's face and knocked him into the wall. His body slumped over and blood leaked out of his mouth.

With every ounce of will left in him, Drake focused on the doctor, but the doctor fought Drake with his own mind powers... and pulled the trigger.

Two pops reverberated through the hall. Sam screamed and Drake unleashed more fury than he'd ever felt before.

Images of his New Daddy flashed through his mind. The gun in the doctor's hand lifted and pointed toward his chin.

"Shoot yourself, Dr. Pana. Don't miss."

Sam's voice cut through the pulsing vibrations in his ears. "Drake no! Don't do it! Don't become one of them."

Drake looked to her, tears welling in his eyes. "I can't lose you, Sam. I lost them. I can't lose you too. I'm sorry."

The doctor's face contorted in fear and rage, but his finger obeyed Drake's will and pulled the trigger. Just like the childhood memory, blood and brain splattered the wall and the doctor's body fell to the floor like a bag of sand.

CHAPTER 25 – SAM

I heard the gun explode in slow motion. Everything went silent, or really loud. I couldn't tell—like when water is so hot it feels cold for a moment. My ears rang as I went numb and fell to the ground. Blood covered me, and my arm stung.

Drake's mouth moved, but I couldn't hear what he said. Rage overtook him, and he turned to the doctor. He broke from my mind and unleashed all his power.

Dr. Pana brought the gun to his own chin. Time slowed. The doctor's finger tugged against the trigger.

"Drake no! Don't do it! Don't become one of them." The words didn't reach my ears. Maybe I only spoke in my head. Nothing made sense. I couldn't move. Something pinned me down.

Drake looked to me, tears in his eyes. "I can't lose you, Sam. I lost them. I can't lose you too. I'm sorry."

My mind filled with Drake's. His pain became mine, his memories my memories. We existed as one in that terrible moment.

The doctor's head exploded in a splash of blood and brain.

I blocked the image of him from my mind, and my connection to Drake snapped shut. The guard still lay unconscious in the corner, and Ana lay like a dead weight against me.

I shifted her, and screamed. A crimson gash covered her abdomen. I tried to move my arm and flinched. Blood covered my right shoulder. Two bullets — one in her, and one that just grazed me. She must have moved at the last minute, and thrown herself in front of me.

She'd saved my life.

This plan was supposed to be simple. How could this happen?

My hearing returned as I choked on my sobs. I held Ana and rocked her, stared at her, willing her to wake up. I waited for that movie moment when she would open her eyes and tell me it was okay, that it was best this way. When she would make me vow to help her children and all the other kids in this hellhole.

That moment never came.

I was robbed of those last words, that final connection.

Images of Gar's lifeless eyes plagued me. Two deaths.

I looked at my bloodstained hands and cringed. I would never wipe my soul clean from this.

"Sam, we have to go now. I'm sorry, but we don't have much time to get out of here. Are you okay? Is our baby okay?"

I stared at Drake, still in a daze, and nodded mutely as he moved Ana's body off of me. "We can't leave her here. That's not right."

"I know, but we have no choice. We're the only hope left to save her kids. She'd want us to go."

"No! I'm not going to leave her here. Her kids deserve to know where she's buried. She deserves some respect. I will not leave her in the hands of these monsters! Not like I left Gar."

"Please, Sam, listen to me. For the sake of our baby, we have to go. Please!"

"I can't. I just can't. The babies. Ana. I can't."

I sat on the floor, crying, clutching her body in my arms, unable to move, unable to think past the grief that ate away at my soul. She'd given everything for her kids, and for us. Her whole life had been a sacrifice for others. I had just reunited her with her children, gave my best friends their mom back. Now, because of me, they'd lost it all.

Sobs tore out of me. My body shook as my tears spilled onto her lifeless face.

***

'Sam, I am so sorry to do this, but I have to. Sam, you will get up and come with me to the car. You will move quickly.'

My mind emptied. Only a compulsion to do as the voice commanded remained. My body moved reflexively as an unknown arm helped me up and guided me out of the building. Distant alarms sounded, but the compulsion was all that mattered.

I saw the guard and what was left of Dr. Pana as if looking through murky waters.

A thread of anger uncoiled inside me. I despised him. I despised them all. If I could burn the whole building down, I would. These thoughts rose up like bubbles from some buried mind, but I could do nothing but walk forward and get in the car.

We found the blue Honda where Ana said it would be. Drake pulled the backpack out of the trunk, and we jumped in. He drove.

The compulsion disappeared, my mind cleared, and all the memories and feelings flooded back to me. I felt violated, mentally raped. Drake couldn't make eye contact with me, and I couldn't speak to him. My rage wouldn't allow it.

I thought about the babies. What would happen to them? Ana had been the only one who loved them and gave them what they needed. We had destroyed so much tonight—so many lives, so much hope.

My arm throbbed in pain and practicality gradually took over. I checked the bags, trying to focus. Good Ana, she'd left us a first aid kit. I disinfected my bullet wound and wrapped it awkwardly with gauze, also replacing the wrecked bandage Ana had put on me.

"Do you want some help with that? I can pull over and—"

"I can do it myself!"

"Sam, I'm sorry. So sorry. But you would have died. Our baby would have died. I couldn't let you stay there!"

I screamed, "You could have used your physical strength! You could have carried me if you had to. You didn't need to use mind control on me. On me!"

"There was no time. You would have fought. You were injured. And you're pregnant! What would you have done in my situation? Huh? Would you have let me die so I wouldn't get mad at you? Would you have held that ethical line at the expense of my life?"

I refused to look at him or answer.

We drove in silence while I counted our cash. Drake looked over at the money. Ana had left us several thousand dollars, at least, and that didn't count the money I'd squirreled away in my secret box.

He finally broke the silence. "We should dump this car and get something else. The plates are traceable."

I finally looked at the GPS. We were in Montana. I hadn't been far off in my guesses, assuming my school was near the hospital.

We drove in the middle of nowhere, in the middle of the night, in the middle of Big Sky Country. We cruised the long, winding country roads, the only sign of life an occasional road sign.

Drake set the GPS for his apartment in Venice, California, but programmed it for back roads until we could get a new car.

"When and where should we get a new car? I don't see any dealerships around." I did not want to speak to him, but logistics had to be handled.

"As soon as possible. First we should swap the plates with another car. That will buy us time until I can get us to a car lot."

"Fine."

It took us a while to pass anything resembling civilization, but we finally found a parking lot full of cars outside a truck stop. I stayed in the car while Drake made the switch. My first night of freedom and I was already an outlaw. Great.

We kept driving.

I dozed on and off, in pain and sickened by what had happened. Ana's dead face flashed every time I closed my eyes. We drove for hours that first night, stopping for gas and food as infrequently as possible. I stayed in the car, not wanting to alarm anyone with my bloody clothes.

Ten hours of driving exhausted us both. I was surprised we'd stayed on the road so long, after the adrenaline crash from our escape. We pulled into a small motel. I wasn't even sure where we were; everything looked the same after so many miles.

Drake checked us in with cash from the bag.

As soon as we walked into the room, I threw my clothes into a trash bag and jumped into the shower, scrubbing until my skin turned red and raw. I couldn't wash away the memories, but at least I could wash away the blood.

As I washed, Shakespeare's Macbeth ran through my mind:

Out, damn'd spot! out, I say!—One; two: why, then

'tis time to do't.—Hell is murky.—Fie, my lord, fie, a soldier, and

afeard? What need we fear who knows it, when none can call our

pow'r to accompt?—Yet who would have thought the old man to

have had so much blood in him?

So much blood, indeed. Blood spilled for me.

Drake took a shower after me. He came out wearing the sweats and t-shirt Ana had left him. I sat on the double bed in my own sweats and t-shirt and looked through the backpack. The bandaging on my arm slipped. I couldn't get it to stay.

He came over and rewrapped it. We didn't speak. I couldn't even look him in the eyes, but the graze of his skin against mine sent shivers through my body.

We each had clothes to sleep in, undergarments for a few days, and one pair of pants with a few different shirts and sweaters.

I booted up the MacBook and found the memory stick, while he counted the cash.

"Sam, this is $20,000. How could she even have this much money?"

"They probably paid her, right? I mean, they thought they controlled her with her kids, so why wouldn't they pay her? Or maybe she found a way to steal from them. Even better."

I shut up, remembering that I wasn't speaking to him.

It was a lot of money, but without jobs, or IDs, or anything, it wouldn't last long. Still, my eyes filled with tears. Ana had given us so much, and paid for it with her life. And we'd left her there to rot.

The baby kicked, and Drake noticed me holding my stomach.

He sat next to me and swallowed hard. "Can I feel her?"

I nodded and put his large hand over the bump, and she gave another good, strong kick.

He smiled and looked in my eyes. "We got out. We saved her. And we will make it through this. Together. I'm so sorry about what I did, Sam. I swear I'll never do that to you again, but I couldn't let you die!"

Tears rolled off my cheek and onto my shirt. He wiped one away with his finger. I was furious with him, but why? If I could use these powers for what I considered the greater good, why couldn't he? He probably did save our lives. We had to get out of there, and he was right: I would have done the same thing to him if it meant saving him and our baby.

Part of me wanted to stay angry, the part that feared the loss of control, but I was too tired to keep fighting with the only person in the world on my side. I leaned toward him, to put my head on his shoulder, but hesitated. Each moment suspended itself in blown glass—so beautiful, so fragile.

As if sensing my uncertainty, he wrapped his arms around me, and I melted into him as though my body had been made for his.

"Don't ever do it again," I said into his t-shirt.

"I won't, I swear." He held my eyes with his. His breath touched my face and smelled like the mint of his toothpaste.

In that moment, as if sensing my desperate need, or maybe reflecting his own, he leaned into me.

Fire grew between us and poured through us.

The blaze reached our lips as they brushed together, gently at first, soft and tender. Then his tongue split my lips. The taste of his mouth, my fingers digging into his back, his hand sliding into my hair as he pulled me closer—with the ebb and flow of this newfound passion, a craving flared to life deep within my body, something new and forbidden. He traced a line of kisses on my cheek.

I willed time to stop and suspend us in this moment forever, like those blown glass memories.

It didn't feel like a first touch or first kiss, but rather like we'd been apart for too many lifetimes and had finally found each other again. My body recognized his intimately. We fell into each other naturally and without hesitation.

I finally felt home. Free. Safe. Loved.

The computer beeped, reminding us we had work to do.

Drake pushed it away. "It can wait until morning. Now, you need rest, and I need to hold you."

How could I argue when all I wanted in the world was to be wrapped in his arms all night long?

I thought my tears had gone for good, but that night I cried myself to sleep again. This time, my tears fell on the strong shoulders of the man I loved. He held me all night, avoiding my injured shoulder. Words were still too much for us after all the shock, but the contact kept me from falling apart.

***

We woke early the next morning and looked through the computer files, which contained compelling evidence—addresses, pictures, secret documents. Everything we'd need to expose Rent-A-Kid.

Drake grabbed the cell phone and made a call. "Brad, this is Drake. Call me back at this number. It's urgent. I'm in trouble." He hung up.

Money and clothes covered our bed. I thought of Ana and.... *Oh God, I have to tell Lucy and Luke.*

I didn't want to, not after everything. My head split in half.

But we had to.

Drake agreed, and we made the link.

And I had the worst conversation of my life.

Their mother's loss shocked and saddened Lucy and Luke. They'd lost more than just a person they'd only talked to once. They'd lost an idea, a dream of how life might have been. They also feared for their future, understandably so. I had to get them out and protect my baby. I didn't know how, but I would find a way.

We dressed, packed up, and hit the road early, still worried about being followed, or reported, or killed. Minor things.

I took the medicine Ana had left me, and told my baby to be good and stay put for a while longer.

We drove and drove and drove, at last finding a used car lot. We ditched Ana's car and bought the cheapest vehicle that looked like it could go the distance. It didn't help that Drake had no ID. It did help that this guy didn't want to report everything to Uncle Sam. They shook on a deal, and we left with our new ride.

We aimed to get to California by that night, and head straight to his apartment.

I leaned back in my seat and admired Drake as he drove. "What do you think Brad will say about all this?"

"Honestly, I don't know. He's always looked for the next great story, but really has been stuck at the newspaper equivalent of middle management. He gets some local stuff, but nothing hard-hitting. He wants to make his mark, but so far he's just barely making rent."

"Maybe this will be the big break he needs."

"If anyone listens. I have a feeling it won't be that easy to bring down this organization."

Yeah, a group like this didn't cave just because some kids showed up with a memory stick and a story. Still, someone had to listen, to see the pieces that didn't add up and want to investigate further.

If his friend couldn't get our story out into the world, we'd find another way. I had sketches, sensitive information on top government officials, and no identity. That proved something, didn't it? I didn't just make myself disappear. Someone, somewhere, would have to believe us.

Drake squeezed my hand. I turned on the radio and shuffled through the many Christian and country music stations, settling on a Dixie Chicks song. I sang along and tried to forget about my life for a while.

Drake glanced at me. "You have a beautiful voice."

"Thank you." I hesitated. "Drake, I know what I want to name our baby." The thought had been percolating in the back of my mind since the night before, but I wasn't ready to speak about it. Until now.

"I'm pretty sure I don't need to read your mind to know what it is."

"Ana." We said her name together. As a prayer. An offering. A promise.

"Sam, I want you to know... I love you. I know I didn't say it last night, but I do. I always will."

"I love you too."

Right on cue, Lonestar's "Amazed" came on.

"I WANNA SPEND THE REST OF MY LIFE... WITH YOU BY MY SIDE... FOREVER AND EVER...."

I sang, he listened, and we went to meet our future together.

<<<<THE END>>>>

ACKNOWLEDGEMENTS

Writing a book is always a labor of love. Rewriting a book with twice the content when the second book in the series is out… that's a labor of insanity. When *Forbidden Mind* first came out in September 2011, it won the *Forward National Literature Award* for 2nd place in Drama and received praise from many fans and critics. It was a good book.

When *Forbidden Fire*, the sequel, came out in March 2012, it was a much better book, and I realized that I had to rewrite *Forbidden Mind* so that it reflected the same style and quality as *Forbidden Fire*. I also wanted to give my readers more of what they wanted. More Sam, more Drake, just more of everything! This new version is nearly twice as long (though still not a long novel by today's standards) and much more developed than the original, but it took a lot of work to get here. I didn't want to have to rewrite *Forbidden Fire* entirely, beyond a few small additions for synchronicity, so I had to be careful. Also, to make it somewhat easier on my editors, I had to track any my new material. This has been a process, and I have many to thank for this book.

First, thanks to Evolved Publishing for taking on the *Forbidden Trilogy*, and subsequently all of my books, and working so hard to make my work shine. Thank you to Lane Diamond, who had to edit this twice! And to Tony Allen, who worked long hours with me on content editing and line editing to make sure everything made sense and still synched with the second book. You guys are the best editorial team a writer could ask for. Thank you also to Sarah Melville, who designed my awesome covers, created bookmarks of my characters and series and has, without complaint, updated the cover for *Forbidden Mind* when needed. You rock!

A big thanks to my fans, who have already made this book and series such a success, and who share my work and support me as a writer in so many ways. I write these for you and love you all!

I'm also blessed with the most amazing friends who encourage me and bless me in so many ways. Thanks especially to Patti Larsen, for being the fastest and best beta reader ever, to Emlyn Chand for teaching me so much about social media and marketing and for being my twin in so many ways, and to L.M. Stull for being so enthusiastic about my books. These ladies are also awesome authors in their own right. The list of people to thank is endless, but I'm pretty sure no one wants the acknowledgements to be longer than the book itself, so let me just say thank you to everyone who has walked this writerly path with me in one way or another. Each one of you have brought something special to my life.

Most writers have, at one time or another, been told by their family to grow up and get a real job. My parents always told me, "Quit your job and get back to writing so we can retire." Seriously, I have the best parents ever. Also, my brother and sisters have always believed in me and encouraged me. So a huge thank you to my parents, for always believing in me and encouraging me, for sending me to great schools and helping out when I was in a bind, and for the unwavering support in so many ways. I love you so much.

If a person can be judged by the friends they keep, then I would rate pretty high on some scales. I am blessed with the best friends and I want to thank a very special friend in particular. Jan Rippingale has been closer than a friend, closer than a sister, even. She's my *Anam Cara*. Thank you, Jan, for everything.

The list is too long to include here, but you know what you mean to me.

And finally, to my children and, as of the day I wrote this, my very-soon-to-be-husband, Dmytry Karpov—the man I'll be marrying in one week and one day. My little girls put up with a lot while I'm working on a book. To thank them for their patience, I wrote them their own series, The Three Lost Kids, but I also want to thank them here. They are the most amazing children and are often found with a nose buried in a book. Thank you, girls, for being patient while I write, and celebrating when I finish another book.

And Dmytry, what can I say? I'm not sure I could do this without you. You're my writing partner, my life partner, my love and my best friend. You make me laugh and make me dinner and make me rehydrate when I've been at the computer too long. I'm the luckiest woman in the world to have you and our children in my life.

ABOUT THE AUTHOR

Kimberly Kinrade was born with ink in her veins and magic in her heart. As a child, where others saw shapes in clouds, she saw words. But she was also an entrepreneur at heart. So when her business arrangement with the Tooth Fairy ended, she went pro by writing her fantastical stories and selling them to all her neighbors.

Fast forward... um... many years and many college degrees later... and she is now a published author after a long career as a journalist and freelance writer.

Though she has written in many genres and fields, she's most passionate about the world of the paranormal and fantasy.

Check out her children's fantasy series at http://ThreeLostKids.com and enjoy **The Three Lost Kids Trilogy:** *Lexie World*, *Bella World* and *Maddie World*.

Also, look for these books coming 2012-2013 from Evolved Publishing:

The Reluctant Familiar (a series): When fate takes hold of her life and thrusts her into a world of gods and goddesses, Agnes must decide: Is she a normal 13 year old girl, or the most powerful witch alive? Coming November 26, 2012.

Blood of the Fallen (a trilogy) co-written with Dmytry Karpov: Luke and Lucy are twins with unusual powers who were raised in secret as paranormal spies.

Once freed from their past, they move to Washington, D.C., for college a fresh start. But will their new job allow for a normal life? Or will their future hold more surprises than they expected? Coming March 19, 2013.

When Kimberly's not writing, editing and writing some more, she spends her time with her three little girls who think they are princess ninjas with hidden supernatural powers, her two dogs who think they are human, and the one man who is her soul mate and writing partner.

Find her at KimberlyKinrade.com

On Twitter

https://twitter.com/#!/kimberlykinrade

On Facebook

http://www.facebook.com/KimberlyKinrade

And subscribe to her newsletter for special deals, perks, and a free copy of the duology *Sunrise & Nightfall* when it launches. *Two Novellas, One Story. Danika Star is dying. Andriy Zorin will live forever. Together, they must face mortality and discover the redemptive power of love.*

~~~~~

If you enjoyed this book, consider supporting the author by leaving a review wherever you purchased this book. Thank you.

WHAT'S NEXT

**FORBIDDEN FIRE (Forbidden Trilogy, Book 2)
By Kimberly Kinrade**

She escaped, but she'll never be free.

"Time held no meaning as my mind darted in and out of memories. Past and present collided to create a full-sensory collage out of my life: playing hide-n-seek with my best friends Luke — who always cheated by walking through walls when he was about to be caught — and Lucy; Mr. Caldrin critiquing my sketches and offering ideas to make them more realistic; targets changing faces, blending into the same person, their thoughts rippling through my

mind like waves. Through it all, a demon stalked me from the shadows of my memories, never quite showing its face, but crouching, waiting.

And then I dreamed...."

~~~~~

Sam and Drake may have escaped, but they aren't free—not with a powerful Seeker after them. As Sam struggles with the ethics of her new powers and embraces a blossoming physical relationship with Drake, Lucy and Luke face challenges of their own.

With forces coalescing inside and outside the Rent-A-Kid dorms, it's only a matter of time before the fire they started forces each of them to make choices they can't undo. But will it be enough to save them?

~~~~~

Get Forbidden Fire on Amazon. Keep reading for an excerpt from Chapter 1.

Chapter 1 – Sam

The warmth of Drake's lips against mine sent butterflies spiraling through my stomach. His strong arms tightened around me just enough to make me feel safe without stealing all the air from my lungs. I rested my cheek against his chest and breathed in his unique scent—part campfire, part wind. Everything about that moment in our bed felt right... until the butterflies in my stomach turned into angry bees bent on killing me.

My legs itched as if unseen bugs crawled through them; I couldn't keep them still. Hot and cold, my body fluctuated between extremes as I opened my mouth to speak, but my throat refused to comply.

"*Drake!*" My mind called to him even as my body pushed away from his.

He held onto me and refused to let me crawl into my own misery. "Sam, what's wrong?"

I tried to speak out loud, but couldn't. "*I don't know. Something is happening to me. Something isn't... right.*"

Drops of sweat trickled down my forehead and stung my eyes. I shivered and clutched at Drake. My hands wrapped around his taut muscles as if trying to absorb their strength.

His hand dropped to my swollen belly, and he switched to our mind link. '*Is it our baby?*'

My mental whimper made me cringe, but I couldn't help it. My body had been invaded by aliens. I wanted to tear my skin off and crawl out of myself. A ball of anxiety grew in my chest, smothering any of the peace I had felt just moments before. "*It's not my stomach, it's everywhere. Like a poison or... Ahhhh!*"

The pain that ripped through me swallowed up all thoughts of words. If I hadn't already been lying in bed with Drake, I would have crashed to the floor. A vague need clawed at me—some unnamable craving that made no sense to my mind, but which captured the needs of my body.

Some *thing* was missing, and its absence sent my nervous system into chaos.

Drake covered me with a blanket, and pressed his cool hand against my head as he brushed long, sweaty strands of dark hair from my eyes. "I'm really freaking out here, Sam. You're pale, clammy, and you can't stop shaking. I don't know what to do. I think I should take you to the hospital." The skin around his blue eyes tightened in worry.

I spoke through chattering teeth. "You can't. Baby. Experiments. They might take me away."

I couldn't summon enough clarity to tell him why this was such a bad idea. I'd spent my whole life in a lie. The people who'd raised me as a paranormal spy, for hire to the rich and powerful, had given me everything any girl would ever need to live comfortably. Then they burned my artwork, killed my mentor, impregnated me against my will and held me prisoner.

If it hadn't been for Drake, I'd have never gotten out. As it was, two people died trying to help me escape.

Drake and I met telepathically, after they kidnapped and imprisoned him at my school. We fell in love before ever meeting in person. Through him, I had learned not only to read minds, but to control them—a gift I often wished I could give back. But it had saved us.

We were free, but hunted.

We couldn't go to a hospital, where we might be reported or discovered. It was too risky.

I didn't realize he'd gone until he came back with a cool washcloth and pressed it against my forehead. "If you aren't feeling better soon, we're going to the doctor's. I'll do whatever it takes to keep you safe and get you out of there, if it comes to that." He towered over me, his spiky blond hair disheveled from our recent make-out session that now seemed so long ago.

My body shuddered, and not just because of my symptoms. *Whatever it takes* could mean a lot of things to Drake, including—but not limited to—physical violence and total mind control. The darkness of his paranormal talents scared me and seduced me in equal measure.

***

Time held no meaning as my mind darted in and out of memories. Past and present collided to create a full-sensory collage out of my life: playing hide-n-seek with my best friends Luke—who always cheated by walking through walls when he was about to be caught—and Lucy; Mr. Caldrin critiquing my sketches and offering ideas to make them more realistic; targets changing faces, blending into the same person, their thoughts rippling through my mind like waves. Through it all, a demon stalked me from the shadows of my memories, never quite showing its face, but crouching, waiting.

And then I dreamed....

***

The needle plunges into me, tearing through skin in one small, sharp poke. Yellow fluid drains from the vial and into my veins.

I float outside my body, above a younger version of myself sitting on the hospital bed. My brown hair is longer, a child's cut with blunted bangs and pigtails. My blue eyes look brighter, more innocent. "Why do I have to get this all the time? What does it do?"

Dr. Sato also looks younger, though very old to my child-self, her Asian features smooth and pronounced, her white coat and stilted accent forever the same. "You not get it all the time. Only every three months. It vitamin. It make you strong and healthy. Make you feel good."

I struggle to slip into her thoughts, but they're all mumbo-jumbo, the sounds foreign and harsh to my young mind. I haven't yet learned many other languages, just one or two common ones. Her Japanese dialect is not common, and no amount of mind reading will change the fact that I cannot understand her words. Trying only gives me a headache.

Then it's okay. I don't mind not knowing, not hearing her thoughts. All is well.

Time slips forward and again I'm in a hospital bed, only this time I'm older... and unconscious. My legs are spread. My sleeping form does not move.

A male doctor I've never seen sticks something inside me —

I scream. And scream. And scream.

No one hears.

***

"Sam. Sam!"

Fingers dug into my shoulders, pulling me from my dream fragments. Ghostly hands clawed at my mind and tried to carry me back into my nightmares, but Drake's hold on me didn't waver. His mind probed mine; my consciousness had no choice but to wake up and take control.

My throat cracked when I spoke. "How long have I been asleep?"

He sat at the edge of the bed and kissed my head. "A few hours."

"I feel worse than before I slept, like I ran a marathon with a hangover."

The right side of his lips curved up in his signature half grin. "You've never had a hangover, so how would you know?"

I smirked. "I don't have to get drunk to know the aftermath doesn't feel so great. Intelligent people learn lessons without having to make all the mistakes. Unlike some, who think that chugging beer through—what do you call those things? Beer hats?—is a genius thing to do."

"That's the last time I tell you any of my secrets."

"Uh... I can read your mind."

"True. Speaking of reading minds... yours was screaming at me while you slept. Then you actually screamed. What were you dreaming, Hon?"

Only bits and pieces of my dream remained–the terror, the invasiveness–but no real details. Something nudged at the back of my memory, though, an important piece of the puzzle that my subconscious mind needed me to remember.

"I think I'm hungry. Or thirsty. Or... something." What? What did I need to feel better? I resisted the urge to scratch the skin off my restless legs, but it was so hard. Everything ached. Everything had a wrongness about it.

Drake left to get me food. I forced myself out of our Queen-sized bed and made my way to the bathroom we shared with Brad. Sharing a bathroom with two men was not the highlight of my new life, but we were lucky Brad had a place for us at all. He'd even kept all of Drake's stuff when he left their old apartment and rented this one. I would forever be grateful to Brad for standing by Drake the way he had all these years.

I wiped down the sink with a piece of toilet paper, erasing evidence of men who brushed their teeth like children, and splashed warm water over my face. My symptoms were all so muddled–pregnancy and illness duking it out for supremacy in my miserable body. *Dizziness. Restless legs. Nausea. Anxiety. Shakiness.* Those all seemed new. Well, not the nausea, but what had once been run-of-the-mill had turned into a Code Red vomit fest. Not normal.

Time for Google.

When Drake returned with a turkey sandwich, a salad and water, I sat propped-up in bed with the laptop on my legs.

My search results revealed a lot of random diagnosis. Adrenal insufficiency. Environmental allergy. Hormone imbalance—*very likely, all things considered.* Unknown pathogen—*thank you, Google, that's very useful.*

The one diagnosis that kept popping up again and again was the one that scared me the most, and made the most sense.

Drug withdrawal.

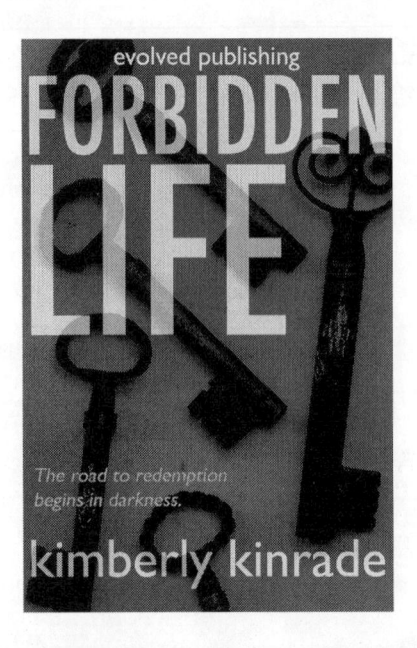

**FORBIDDEN LIFE (Forbidden Trilogy, Book 3)
By Kimberly Kinrade**

The road to redemption begins in darkness.

The older Rent-A-Kids are free, but a powerful force still pulses in the darkness, keeping them all prisoners to their power.

With Drake gone and her power spiraling out of control, Sam doesn't know how she'll make it through the birth of her child—or how she'll protect that child from the evil that stalks her.

Drake will do anything to get his powers back... but when his choices lead to drugs and secrets, he has to decide what he's willing to lose forever.

Lucy's shadow powers are growing stronger—too strong. As she and Luke work with the mysterious I.P.I. agents to free the babies and young children still held captive at Rent-A-Kid, Lucy must make some difficult decisions that could jeopardize her friendships, and their mission.

In this final installment of the award-winning Forbidden trilogy, each character must conquer their darkest demons or lose everything in this final battle against the evil Rent-A-Kid organization.

~~~~~

Coming October 2, 2012 from Evolved Publishing.

Add *Forbidden Life* on Goodreads.

THE RELUCTANT FAMILIAR
(The Reluctant Familiar – Book 1)

Shamed by her family.

A disgrace to witches everywhere.

Agnes must decide:

Is she a normal 13-year-old-girl, or the most powerful witch alive?

After a seemingly chance encounter with a flea-ridden alley cat finds her bonded to a god and in possession of powers she has no control over, life is anything but normal.

As if that's not enough to upset a girl's day, a powerful ring has been stolen, and Agnes and Sebastian are the only hope for getting it back and saving the world from the crazed plans of a powerful deity.

If they succeed, they will each get their heart's desire.

But if they fail, death will be their only reward.

~~~~~

Look for it November 26, 2012 through Evolved Publishing.

Cover art by Sam Keiser.

Add it on Goodreads.

Other Novels From Evolved Publishing
www.EvolvedPub.com

Childrens' Picture Books
Honey the Hero (Emlyn Chand)

Fantasy/ScienceFiction
Eulogy (D.T Conklin)

Historical
Circles (Ruby Standing Deer)

Literary Fiction
Torn Together* (Emlyn Chand)
Jellicle Girl* (Stevie Mikayne)

Memoir
And Then it Rained: Lessons for Life
(Megan Morrison)

Romance
Her Twisted Pleasures (Amelia James)
Tell Me You Want Me (Amelia James)

Thriller/Suspense
Forgive Me, Alex (Lane Diamond)

Young Adult
Dead Radiance (T.G Ayer)
Desert Rice* (Angela Scott)
Fall Back* (Emlyn Chand)
The Silver Sphere* (Michael Dadich)
Wanted: Dead or Undead (Angela Scott)

*Coming soon from Evolved Publishing

Made in the USA
Charleston, SC
19 November 2012